FIRST CONTACT

HE SHADED HIS EYES FROM THE SUN AND LOOKED OFF toward the village. "This isn't exactly what I expected."

"What did you expect, Sambeke?" I asked.

"I thought you people were trying to create a Utopia here."

"We are."

He snorted contemptuously. "You live in huts, you have no machinery, and you even have to hire someone from Earth to kill hyenas for you. That's not *my* idea of Utopia."

"Then you will doubtless wish to return to your home," I suggested.

"I have a job to do here first," he replied. "A job *you* failed to do."

I made no answer, and he stared at me for a long moment.

"Well?" he said at last.

"Well what?"

"Aren't you going to spout some mumbo-jumbo and make me disappear in a cloud of smoke, *mundumugu*?"

"Before you choose to become my enemy," I said in perfect English, "you should know that I am not as ineffectual as you may think, nor am I impressed by Maasai arrogance."

He stared at me in surprise, then threw back his head and laughed.

"There's more to you than meets the eye, old man!" he said in English. "I think we are going to become great friends!"

"I doubt it," I replied in Swahili.

Other Tor titles by Mike Resnick

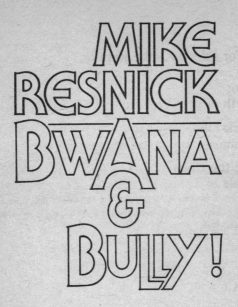

MIKE RESNICK
BWANA & BULLY!

A TOM DOHERTY ASSOCIATES BOOK
NEW YORK

Tor SF Double No. 33

BWANA

BULLY!

A Tor Book
Published by Tom Doherty Associates, Inc.
49 West 24th Street
New York, N.Y. 10010

Cover art by Barclay Shaw

ISBN: 0-812-51246-4

First edition: June 1991

Printed in the United States of America

9 8 7 6 5 4 3 2 1

INTRODUCTION

ALMOST ALL SCIENCE FICTION WRITERS, NO MATTER WHAT their politics, share one basic belief: that if we can reach the stars, we'll colonize them. This in turn leads to the not-unlikely supposition that, somewhere along the way, we're going to come into contact—and eventually into cultural conflict—with alien races.

But (I hear you say) science fiction is supposed to be based on fact. So where does a science fiction writer go to study the effects of colonization and cultural conflict—Mars? Venus? Alpha Centauri?

Well, maybe someday. But right now there is a remarkable continent that offers not one, not two, but fully half a hundred examples of the effects of colonization on both the colonizers and the colonized. I'm speaking of Africa, of course, and for those of you who think it isn't really filled with alien cultures, I invite you to examine it more closely.

You want a truly alien society? Forget about Mesklin and Barsoom, and turn your eyes to Kenya.

Here is a modern, 20th-Century nation, totally capitalistic, with its very own metropolis (Nairobi, population 1.5 million) and a number of sophisticated industries.

But not a single one of Kenya's 40-plus tribes had a word for "wheel" in 1900.

Not one of them entered the 20th Century with a written language.

There is no word for "woman" in Swahili. The closest you can come is "manamouki," which means female property, and applies equally to women, sows, cows, bitches, and mares.

90% of the population claims to be Christian, but 80% see their witch doctor far more often than their minister or priest.

80% of all Kenyans of *both* sexes still undergo circumcision ceremonies as teenagers.

English is the official language of Kenya; less than 5% of the population can speak it.

You think you can't transfer that society to Planet X and get a couple of serious extrapolations out of it?

Or try Uganda. Everybody knows about Idi Amin—but how many people know that Dr. Milton Obote, who succeeded him, killed even more Ugandans than Amin? Or that General Okello, who overthrew Obote, also killed more of his own countrymen than Amin?

What kind of society, once considered "the pearl of Africa" by no less a statesman than Winston

Churchill, can produce three such genocidal maniacs in succession?

How can there *not* be a science fiction novel or two in a society that continually lines up to be slaughtered by its own leaders?

Then there's South Africa, with a white minority practicing *apartheid* on a continent where its 44 closest neighbors are ruled by their black majorities—and suddenly, in 1990, trying to convince 3 generations of thoroughly brainwashed whites that *apartheid* is a bad thing after all.

You think you can't translate *that* into a grim novel of human xenophobia in a galaxy where we're outnumbered hundreds to one?

How about Tanzania? Here's a country run by perhaps the most brilliant socialist philosopher of this century, Julius Nyerere, whose greatest tragedy is that he didn't have a better country to practice with. No matter what innovation he tried, no matter what lever he pulled, his country was just too poor and barren to respond to his vision, and in the end he bankrupted it, putting the final financial nail in the coffin by being literally the only leader on the continent who was willing to oppose Idi Amin.

Hard science, soft science, politics, human tragedy—what more could a science fiction writer want than a world drawn from Tanzania?

You want alien customs? Try "Sharia". This is the name of the Islamic custom/law, still being practiced, that allows the victim's next of kin or family to decide what punishment is meted out to his killer in the Sudan. Included among the choices are crucifixion and boiling in oil.

Nor is Africa's sordid history of slavery a closed

book. Even today there are an estimated 20,000 Dinka slaves in the Sudan, and an estimated 100,000 slaves are sold, continent-wide, per year, usually to other Africans.

How much more alien can you get?

So, a few years ago, I started carving out chunks of the African landscape and finding ways to use them in my science fiction.

Bits and pieces appeared here and there. Chapter 5 of *The Soul Eater* is a hunt for alien beasts, set in a thinly-disguised analog of Tanzania's Ngorongoro Crater. The protagonist was named for an old-time African trader, and the bartender for a Zulu chieftain. Chapter 23 of *Birthright: The Book of Man*, the future history of the human race in which the majority of my novels have been set, takes place in a future version of an ecologically degraded Serengeti, a vast land devoid of all animal life.

Nobody screamed foul, so I continued borrowing little parts of Africa for the *Tales of the Galactic Midway* series and for *Santiago*.

Finally I decided it was time to take the plunge and borrow more than a little bit here and a little bit there.

My first attempt was *Adventures*, a parody of every bad pulp story and B movie ever set on the Dark Continent.

Then came *The Dark Lady*, in which the story had nothing to do with Africa, but was told by an alien who had to function in a xenophobic human society, courtesy of P. Botha and his henchmen.

Then I wrote *Ivory*, in which I took an historical artifact—the record tusks of the Kilimanjaro Elephant, who was killed under mysterious circumstances in 1898—and created an epic that spanned eight millennia. It was nominated for both the Nebula and the Clarke awards, which encouraged me to keep mining this rich vein of source material.

Next came *Paradise*, probably my best novel to date, which is an allegory of Kenya's history from 1890 to 2010.

And, starting in 1988 and continuing over the next few years, there are the "Kirinyaga" stories, which seem to have done more for my reputation than all my novels, and which chronicle the attempts, as told by an old witch doctor, to preserve a traditional Kikuyu society in the face of 21st Century technology. The first one, "Kirinyaga," won the Hugo and was a Nebula nominee; the second, "For I Have Touched the Sky," was both a Hugo and Nebula nominee. "Bwana," which you hold in your hands, is the third in the series; three more have been written and sold, and when the dust clears there will be ten in all.

By the time 1990 rolled around, I found, to my surprise, that I was an acknowledged expert on the growing sub-genre of African science fiction (but far from the only one, I hasten to point out: read the recent works of George Alec Effinger, Michael Bishop, and Robert Silverberg, to name just three others who have recently produced major works of science fiction set in Africa).

Anyway, while tossing around ideas to interest the audience that seems to have developed for such stories, I got to wondering what might have happened had Africa been colonized not by the royalists or the imperialists, but by an American who felt that he could learn from Europe's mistakes and could bring good old American know-how and democratic values to a harsh, savage land.

I have always found Teddy Roosevelt to be the most fascinating American of this century. Most people know him only as a jingoist, or a pudgy lampoon who cries "Charge!" as he runs up the stairs in *Arsenic and Old Lace*, but the historical Roosevelt was anything but a figure of fun: as a teenager, he was considered to be among the most knowledgeable taxidermists and ornithologists in America; he graduated Harvard with outstanding grades, and was the leader of the New York Republican Party at the ripe young age of 25; he was the most efficient Police Commissioner New York City ever had, and as a deputy sheriff in the Dakota Bad Lands he went out, unarmed, after three killers in a terrible blizzard and brought them in; he was a best-selling author, an authentic war hero, a splendid governor, a remarkably effective president, and a world-class explorer who even has a river named after him.

What if I used Teddy as my colonist? (He actually was invited to do just that; the excerpts at the beginning of the story are authentic.) How would this most competent of Americans have fared? Would Africa be appreciably different if we had taken a hand in its colonization?

Well, when you're through with *Bwana*, turn to *Bully!* and you'll find one writer's answer.

—Mike Resnick

BWANA

To Carol, as always

And to Patrick Nielsen Hayden,
a fine, hard-working, and patient editor
who puts up with a lot (especially from me)

NGAI RULES THE UNIVERSE FROM HIS THRONE ATOP KIRIN-yaga, which men call Mount Kenya, and on His sacred mountain the beasts of the field roam free and share the fertile green slopes with His chosen people.

To the first Maasai He gave a spear, and to the first Kamba He gave a bow, but to Gikuyu, who was the first Kikuyu, He gave a digging stick and told him to dwell on the slopes of Kirinyaga. The Kikuyu, said Ngai, could sacrifice goats to read their entrails, and they could sacrifice oxen to thank Him for sending the rains, but they must not molest any of His animals that dwelt on the mountain.

Then one day Gikuyu came to Him and said, "May we not have the bow and arrow, so that we may kill *fisi*, the hyena, in whose body dwell the vengeful souls of evil men?"

And Ngai said that no, the Kikuyu must not molest the hyena, for the hyena's purpose was clear: He had created it to feed upon the lions' leavings, and to take the sick and the elderly from the Kikuyus' *shambas*.

Time passed, and Gikuyu approached the summit of the mountain again. "May we not have the spear, so that we can kill the lion and the leopard, who prey upon our own animals?" he said.

And Ngai said that no, the Kikuyu could not kill the lion or the leopard, for He had created them to hold the population of the grasseaters in check, so that they would not overrun the Kikuyus' fields.

Finally Gikuyu climbed the mountain one last time and said, "We must at least be allowed to kill the elephant, who can destroy a year's harvest in a matter of minutes—but how are we to do so when you have allowed us no weapons?"

Ngai thought long and hard, and finally spoke. "I have decreed that the Kikuyu should till the land, and I will not stain your hands with the blood of my other creatures," announced Ngai. "But because you are my chosen people, and are more important than the beasts that dwell upon my mountain, I will see to it that others come to kill these animals."

"What tribe will these hunters come from?" asked Gikuyu. "By what name will we know them?"

"You will know them by a single word," said Ngai.

When Ngai told him the word by which the hunters would be known, Gikuyu thought He had made a joke, and laughed aloud, and soon forgot the conversation.

But Ngai never jokes when He speaks to the Kikuyu.

* * *

We have no elephants or lions or leopards on the Eutopian world of Kirinyaga, for all three species were extinct long before we emigrated from the Kenya that had become so alien to us. But we took the sleek impala, and the majestic kudu, and the mighty buffalo, and the swift gazelle—and because we were mindful of Ngai's dictates, we took the hyena and the jackal and the vulture as well.

And because Kirinyaga was designed to be a Utopia in climate as well as in social organization, and because the land was more fertile than Kenya's, and because Maintenance made the orbital adjustments that assured us that the rains would always come on schedule, the wild animals of Kirinyaga, like the domestic animals and the people themselves, grew fruitful and multiplied.

It was only a matter of time before they came into conflict with us. Initially there would be sporadic attacks on our livestock by the hyenas, and once old Koboki's entire harvest was destroyed by a herd of rampaging buffalo, but we took such setbacks with good grace, for Ngai had provided well for us and no one was ever forced to go hungry.

But then, as we reclaimed more and more of our terraformed veldt to be used as farmland, and as the wild animals of Kirinyaga felt the pressure of our land-hungry people, the incidents grew more frequent and more severe.

I was sitting before the fire in my *boma*, waiting for the sun to burn the chill from the morning air and staring out across the acacia-dotted plains, when young Ndemi raced up the winding road from the village.

"Koriba!" he cried. "Come quickly!"

"What has happened?" I asked, rising painfully to my feet.

"Juma has been attacked by *fisi*!" he gasped, striving to regain his breath.

"By one hyena, or many?" I asked.

"One, I think. I do not know."

"Is he still alive?"

"Juma or *fisi*?" asked Ndemi.

"Juma."

"I think he is dead." Ndemi paused. "But you are the *mundumugu*. You can make him live again."

I was pleased that he placed so much faith in his *mundumugu*—his witch doctor—but of course if his companion was truly dead there was nothing I could do about it. I went into my hut, selected some herbs that were especially helpful in combatting infection, added a few *qat* leaves for Juma to chew (for we had no anesthetics on Kirinyaga, and the hallucinogenic trance caused by the *qat* leaves would at least make him forget his pain). All this I placed into a leather pouch that I hung about my neck. Then I emerged from my hut and nodded to Ndemi, who led the way to the *shamba* of Juma's father.

When we arrived, the women were already wailing the death chant, and I briefly examined what was left of poor little Juma's body. One bite from the hyena had taken away most of his face, and a second had totally removed his left arm. The hyena had then devoured most of Juma's torso before the villagers finally drove it away.

Koinnage, the paramount chief of the village, arrived a few moments later.

"*Jambo*, Koriba," he greeted me.

"*Jambo*, Koinnage," I replied.

"Something must be done," he said, looking at Juma's body, which was now covered by flies.

"I will place a curse on the hyena," I said, "and tonight I shall sacrifice a goat to Ngai, so that He will welcome Juma's soul."

Koinnage looked uneasy, for his fear of me was great, but finally he spoke: "It is not enough. This is the second healthy boy that the hyenas have taken this month."

"Our hyenas have developed a taste for men," I said. "It is because we leave the old and the infirm out for them."

"Then perhaps we should not leave the old and the sick out any longer."

"We have no choice," I replied. "The Europeans thought it was the mark of savages, and even Maintenance has tried to dissuade us—but we do not have medicine to ease their suffering. What seems barbarous to outsiders is actually an act of mercy. Ever since Ngai gave the first digging-stick to the first Kikuyu, it has always been our tradition to leave the old and the infirm out for the hyenas when it is time for them to die."

"Maintenance has medicines," suggested Koinnage, and I noticed that two of the younger men had edged closer to us and were listening with interest. "Perhaps we should ask them to help us."

"So that they will live a week or a month longer, and then be buried in the ground like Christians?" I said. "You can not be part Kikuyu and part European. That is the reason we came to Kirinyaga in the first place."

"But how wrong could it be to ask only for medicine for our elderly?" asked one of the younger men, and I could see that Koinnage looked relieved now that he himself did not have to pursue the argument.

"If you accept their medicine today, then tomorrow you will be accepting their clothing and their machinery and their god," I replied. "If history has taught us nothing else, it has taught us that." They still seemed unconvinced, so I continued: "Most races look ahead to their Utopia, but the Kikuyu must look *back*, back to a simpler time when we lived in harmony with the land, when we were not tainted with the customs of a society to which we were never meant to belong. I have lived among the Europeans, and gone to school at their universities, and I tell you that you must not listen to the siren song of their technology. What works for Europeans did not work for the Kikuyu when we lived in Kenya, and it will not work for us here on Kirinyaga."

As if to emphasize my statement, a hyena voiced its eerie laugh far off in the veldt. The women stopped wailing and drew closer together.

"But we must do something!" protested Koinnage, whose fear of the hyena momentarily overrode his fear of his *mundumugu*. "We cannot continue to let the beasts of the field destroy our crops and take our children."

I could have explained that there was a temporary imbalance as the grasseaters lowered their birthrate to accommodate their decreased pasturage, and that the hyenas' birthrate would almost certainly adjust within a year, but they would not have understood or believed me. They wanted solutions, not explanations.

"Ngai is testing our courage, to see if we are truly worthy to live on Kirinyaga," I said at last. "Until the time of testing is over, we will arm our children with spears and have them tend the cattle in pairs."

Koinnage shook his head. "The hyenas have developed a taste for men—and two Kikuyu boys, even armed with spears, are no match for a pack of hyenas. Surely Ngai does not want His chosen people to become meals for *fisi*."

"No, He does not," I agreed. "It is the hyenas' nature to kill grasseaters, just as it is our nature to till the fields. I am your *mundumugu*. You must believe me when I tell you that this time of testing will soon pass."

"How soon?" asked another man.

I shrugged. "Perhaps two rains. Perhaps three." The rains come twice a year.

"You are an old man," said the man, mustering his courage to contradict his *mundumugu*. "You have no children, and it is this that gives you patience. But those of us with sons cannot wait for two or three rains wondering each day if they will return from the fields. We must do something *now*."

"I am an old man," I agreed, "and this gives me not only patience, but wisdom."

"You are the *mundumugu*," said Koinnage at last, "and you must face the problem in your way. But I am the paramount chief, and I must face it in mine. I will organize a hunt, and we will kill all the hyenas in the area."

"Very well," I said, for I had foreseen this solution. "Organize your hunt."

"Will you cast the bones and see if we shall be successful?"

"I do not need to cast the bones to foresee the results of your hunt," I replied. "You are farmers, not hunters. You will not be successful."

"You will not give us your support?" demanded another man.

"You do not need my support," I replied. "I would give you my patience if I could, for that is what you need."

"We were supposed to turn this world into a Utopia," said Koinnage, who had only the haziest understanding of the word, but equated it with good harvests and a lack of enemies. "What kind of Utopia permits children to be devoured by wild animals?"

"You cannot understand what it means to be full until you have been hungry," I answered. "You cannot know what it means to be warm and dry until you have been cold and wet. And Ngai knows, even if you do not, that you cannot appreciate life without death. This is His lesson for you; it will pass."

"It must end *now*," said Koinnage firmly, now that he knew I would not try to prevent his hunt.

I made no further comment, for I knew that nothing I could say would dissuade him. I spent the next few minutes creating a curse for the individual hyena that had killed Juma, and that night I sacrificed a goat in the middle of the village and read in the entrails that Ngai had accepted the sacrifice and welcomed Juma's spirit.

Two days later Koinnage led ten of the village men out to the veldt to hunt the hyenas, while I stayed in my *boma* and prepared for what I knew was inevitable.

It was in late morning that Ndemi—the boldest of the boys in the village, whose courage had made him a favorite of mine—came up the long winding path to visit me.

"*Jambo*, Koriba," he greeted me unhappily.

"*Jambo*, Ndemi," I replied. "What is the matter?"

"They say that I am too young to hunt for *fisi*," he complained, squatting down next to me.

"They are right."

"But I have practiced my bushcraft every day, and you yourself have blessed my spear."

"I have not forgotten," I said.

"Then why can I not join the hunt?"

"It makes no difference," I said. "They will not kill *fisi*. In fact, they will be very lucky if all of them return unharmed." I paused. "*Then* the troubles will begin."

"I thought they had already begun," said Ndemi, with no trace of sarcasm.

I shook my head. "What has been happening is part of the natural order of things, and hence it is part of Kirinyaga. But when Koinnage does not kill the hyenas, he will want to bring a hunter to Kirinyaga, and that is *not* part of the natural order."

"You know he will do this?" asked Ndemi, impressed.

"I know Koinnage," I answered.

"Then you will tell him not to."

"I will tell him not to."

"And he will listen to you."

"No," I said. "I do not think he will listen to me."

"But you are the *mundumugu*."

"But there are many men in the village who resent me," I explained. "They see the sleek ships that land on Kirinyaga from time to time, and they hear stories about the wonders of Nairobi and Mombasa, and they forget why we have come here. They become unhappy with the digging-stick, and they long for the Maasai's spear or the Kamba's bow or the European's machines."

Ndemi squatted in silence for a moment.

"I have a question, Koriba," he said at last.

"You may ask it."

"You are the *mundumugu*," he said. "You can change men into insects, and see in the darkness, and walk upon the air."

"That is true," I agreed.

"Then why do you not turn all the hyenas into honeybees and set fire to their hive?"

"Because *fisi* is not evil," I said. "It is his nature to eat flesh. Without him, the beasts of the field would become so plentiful that they would soon overrun our fields."

"Then why not kill just those *fisi* who kill us?"

"Do you not remember your own grandmother?" I asked. "Do you not recall the agony she suffered in her final days?"

"Yes."

"We do not kill our own kind. Were it not for *fisi*, she would have suffered for many more days. *Fisi* is only doing what Ngai created him to do."

"Ngai also created hunters," said Ndemi, casting me a sly look out of the corner of his eye.

"That is true."

"Then why do you not want hunters to come and kill *fisi*?"

"I will tell you the story of the Goat and the Lion, and then you will understand," I said.

"What do goats and lions have to do with hyenas?" he asked.

14

"Listen, and you will know," I answered. "Once there was a herd of black goats, and they lived a very happy life, for Ngai had provided them with green grass and lush plants and a nearby stream where they could drink, and when it rained they stood beneath the branches of large, stately trees where the raindrops could not reach them. Then one day a leopard came to their village, and because he was old and thin and weak, and could no longer hunt the impala and the waterbuck, he killed a goat and ate it.

" 'This is terrible!' said the goats. 'Something must be done.'

" 'He is an old leopard,' said the wisest of the goats. 'If he regains his strength from the flesh he has eaten, he will go back to hunting the impala, for the impala's flesh is much more nourishing than ours, and if he does not regain his strength, he will soon be dead. All we need do is be especially alert while he walks among us.'

"But the other goats were too frightened to listen to his counsel, and they decided that they needed help.

" 'I would beware of anyone who is not a goat and offers to help you,' said the wisest goat, but they would not hear him, and finally they sought out a huge black-maned lion.

" 'There is a leopard that is eating our people,' they said, 'and we are not strong enough to drive him away. Will you help us?'

" 'I am always glad to help my friends,' answered the lion.

" 'We are a poor race,' said the goats. 'What tribute will you exact from us for your help?'

" 'None,' the lion assured them. 'I will do this solely because I am your friend.'

"And true to his word, the lion entered the village and waited until next the leopard came to feed, and then the lion pounced upon him and killed him.

" 'Oh, thank you, great savior!' cried the goats, doing a dance of joy and triumph around the lion.

" 'It was my pleasure,' said the lion. 'For the leopard is my enemy as much as he is yours.'

" 'We shall sing songs and tell stories about you long after you leave,' continued the goats happily.

" 'Leave?' replied the lion, his eyes seeking out the fattest of the goats. 'Who is leaving?' "

Ndemi considered what I had said for a long moment, then looked up at me.

"You are not saying that the hunter will eat us as *fisi* does?"

"No, I am not."

He considered the implications further.

"Ah!" he said, smiling at last. "You are saying that if we cannot kill *fisi*, who will soon die or leave us, then we should not invite someone even stronger than *fisi*, someone who will not die or leave."

"That is correct."

"But why should a hunter of animals be a threat to Kirinyaga?" he continued thoughtfully.

"We are like the goats," I explained. "We live off the land, and we have not the power to kill our enemies. But a hunter is like the lion: It is his nature to kill, and he will be the only man on Kirinyaga who is skilled at killing."

"You think he will kill us, then?" asked Ndemi.

I shrugged. "Not at first. The lion had to kill the leopard before he could prey upon the goats. The hunter will kill *fisi* before he casts about for some other way to exercise his power."

"But you are our *mundumugu*!" protested Ndemi. "You will not let this happen!"

"I will try to prevent it," I said.

"If you try, you will succeed, and we will not send for a hunter."

"Perhaps."

"Are you not all-powerful?" asked Ndemi.

"I am all-powerful."

"Then why do you speak with such doubt?"

"Because I am not a hunter," I said. "The Kikuyu fear me because of my powers, but I have never knowingly harmed one of my people. I will not harm them now. I want what is best for Kirinyaga, but if their fear of *fisi* is greater than their fear of me, then I will lose."

Ndemi stared at the little patterns he had traced in the dirt with his finger.

"Perhaps, if a hunter does come, he will be a good man," he said at last.

"Perhaps," I agreed. "But he will still be a hunter." I paused. "The lion may sleep with the zebra in times of plenty. But in times of need, when both are starving, it is the lion who starves last."

Ten hunters had left the village, but only eight returned. Two had been attacked and killed by a pack of hyenas while they sat resting beneath the shade of an acacia tree. All day long the women wailed the death chant, while the sky turned black with smoke, for it is our custom to burn the huts of our dead.

That very same night Koinnage called a meeting of the Council of Elders. I waited until the last rays of the sun had vanished, then painted my face and wrapped myself in my ceremonial leopardskin cloak, and made my way to his *boma*.

There was total silence as I approached the old men of the village. Even the night birds seemed to have taken flight, and I walked among them, looking neither right nor left, finally taking my accustomed place on a stool just to the left of Koinnage's personal hut. I could see his three wives clustered together inside his senior wife's hut, kneeling as close to the entrance as they dared while straining to see and hear what transpired.

The flickering firelight highlighted the faces of the elders, most of them grim and filled with fear. By precedent no one—not even the *mundumugu*—could speak until the paramount chief had spoken, and since Koinnage had still not emerged from his hut, I amused myself by withdrawing the bones from the leather pouch about my neck and casting them on the dirt. Three times I cast them, and three times I frowned at what I saw. Finally I put them back in my pouch, leaving those elders who were planning to disobey their *mundumugu* to wonder what I had seen.

At last Koinnage stepped forth from his hut, a long thin stick in his hand. It was his custom to wave the stick when he spoke to the Council, much as a conductor waves his baton.

"The hunt has failed," he announced dramatically, as if everyone in the village did not already know it. "Two more men have died because of *fisi*." He paused for dramatic effect, then shouted: "It must not happen again!"

"Do not go hunting again and it will not happen

again," I said, for once he began to speak I was permitted to comment.

"You are the *mundumugu*," said one of the elders. "You should have protected them!"

"I told them not to go," I replied. "I cannot protect those who reject my counsel."

"*Fisi* must die!" screamed Koinnage, and as he turned to face me I detected a strong odor of *pombe* on his breath, and now I knew why he had remained in his hut for so long. He had been drinking *pombe* until his courage was up to the task at hand, that of opposing his *mundumugu.* "Never again will *fisi* dine upon the flesh of the Kikuyu, nor will we hide in our *bomas* like old women until Koriba tells us that it is safe to come out! *Fisi* must die!"

The elders took up the chant of "*Fisi* must die!" and Koinnage went through a pantomime of killing a hyena, using his stick as a spear.

"Men have reached the stars!" cried Koinnage. "They have built great cities beneath the sea. They have killed the last elephant and the last lion. Are we not men, too—or are we old women, to be terrified by unclean eaters of carrion?"

I got to my feet.

"What other men have achieved makes no difference to the Kikuyu," I said. "Other men did not cause our problem with *fisi*; other men cannot cure it."

"One of them can," said Koinnage, looking at the anxious faces which were distorted by the firelight. "A hunter."

The elders muttered their approval.

"We must send for a hunter," repeated Koinnage, waving his stick wildly.

"It must not be a European," said an elder.

"Nor can it be a Wakamba," said another.

"Nor a Luo," said a third.

"The Nandi are the enemies of our blood," added a fourth.

"It will be whoever can kill *fisi*," said Koinnage.

"How will you find such a man?" asked an elder.

"Hyenas still live on Earth," answered Koinnage. "We will find a hunter or a control officer from one of the game parks, someone who has hunted and killed *fisi* many times."

"You are making a mistake," I said firmly, and suddenly there was absolute silence again.

"We must have a hunter," said Koinnage adamantly, when he saw that no one else would speak.

"You would only be bringing a greater killer to Kirinyaga to slay a lesser killer," I responded.

"I am the paramount chief," said Koinnage, and I could tell from the way he refused to meet my gaze that the effects of the *pombe* had left him now that he was forced to confront me before the elders. "What kind of chief would I be if I permitted *fisi* to continue to kill my people?"

"You can build traps for *fisi* until Ngai gives him back his taste for grasseaters," I said.

"How many more of us will *fisi* kill before the traps have been set?" demanded Koinnage, trying to work himself up into a rage again. "How many of us must die before the *mundumugu* admits that he is wrong, and that this is not Ngai's plan?"

"Stop!" I shouted, raising my hands above my head, and even Koinnage froze in his tracks, afraid to speak or to move. "I am your *mundumugu*. I am the book of our collected wisdom; each sentence I speak is a page. I have brought the rains on time, and I have blessed the harvest. Never have I misled you. Now I tell you that you must not bring a hunter to Kirinyaga."

And then Koinnage, who was literally shaking from his fear of me, forced himself to stare into my eyes.

"I am the paramount chief," he said, trying to steady his voice, "and I say we must act before *fisi* hungers again. *Fisi* must die! I have spoken."

The elders began chanting "*Fisi* must die!" again, and Koinnage's courage returned to him as he realized that he was not the only one to openly disobey his *mundumugu*'s dictates. He led the frenzied chanting, walking from one elder to the next and finally to me, yelling "*Fisi* must die!" and punctuating it with wild gesticulations of his stick.

I realized that I had lost for the very first time in council, yet I made no threats, since it was important that any punishment for disobeying the dictates of their *mundumugu* must come from Ngai and not from me. I left in silence, walking through the circle of elders without looking at any of them, and returned to my *boma*.

The next morning two of Koinnage's cattle were found dead without a mark upon them, and each morning thereafter a different elder awoke to two dead cattle. I told the villagers that this was undoubtedly the hand of Ngai, and that the corpses must be burned, and that anyone who ate of them would die under a horrible *thahu*, or curse, and they followed my orders without question.

Then it was simply a matter of waiting for Koinnage's hunter to arrive.

* * *

He walked across the plain toward my *boma*, and it might have been Ngai Himself approaching me. He was tall, well over six and one-half feet, and slender, graceful as the gazelle and blacker than the darkest night. He was dressed in neither a *kikoi* nor in khakis, but in a lightweight pair of pants and a short-sleeved shirt. His feet were in sandals, and I could tell from the depth of his calluses and the straightness of his toes that he had spent most of his life without shoes. A small bag was slung over one shoulder, and in his left hand he carried a long rifle in a monogrammed gun case.

When he reached the spot where I was sitting he stopped, totally at ease, and stared unblinkingly at me. From the arrogance of his expression, I knew that he was a Maasai.

"Where is the village of Koriba?" he asked in Swahili.

I pointed to my left. "In the valley," I said.

"Why do you live alone, old man?"

Those were his exact words. Not *mzee*, which is a term of respect for the elderly, a term that acknowledges the decades of accumulated wisdom, but *old man*.

Yes, I concluded silently, *there is no doubt that you are a Maasai.*

"The *mundumugu* always lives apart from other men," I answered aloud.

"So you are the witch doctor," he said. "I would have thought your people had outgrown such things."

"As yours have outgrown the need for manners?" I responded.

He chuckled in amusement. "You are not glad to see me, are you, old man?"

"No, I am not."

"Well, if your magic had been strong enough to kill the hyenas, I would not be here. *I* am not to blame for that."

"You are not to blame for anything," I said. "Yet."

"What is your name, old man?"

"Koriba."

He placed a thumb to his chest. "I am William."

"That is not a Maasai name," I noted.

"My full name is William Sambeke."

"Then I will call you Sambeke."

He shrugged. "Call me whatever you want." He shaded his eyes from the sun and looked off toward the village. "This isn't exactly what I expected."

"What did you expect, Sambeke?" I asked.

"I thought you people were trying to create a Utopia here."

"We are."

He snorted contemptuously. "You live in huts, you have no machinery, and you even have to hire someone from Earth to kill hyenas for you. That's not *my* idea of Utopia."

"Then you will doubtless wish to return to your home," I suggested.

"I have a job to do here first," he replied. "A job *you* failed to do."

I made no answer, and he stared at me for a long moment.

"Well?" he said at last.

"Well what?"

"Aren't you going to spout some mumbo-jumbo

and make me disappear in a cloud of smoke, *mundumugu*?"

"Before you choose to become my enemy," I said in perfect English, "you should know that I am not as ineffectual as you may think, nor am I impressed by Maasai arrogance."

He stared at me in surprise, then threw back his head and laughed.

"There's more to you than meets the eye, old man!" he said in English. "I think we are going to become great friends!"

"I doubt it," I replied in Swahili.

"What schools did you attend back on Earth?" he asked, matching my change in languages again.

"Cambridge and Yale," I said. "But that was many years ago."

"Why does an educated man choose to sit in the dirt beside a grass hut?"

"Why does a Maasai accept a commission from a Kikuyu?" I responded.

"I like to hunt," he said. "And I wanted to see this Utopia you have built."

"And now you have seen it."

"I have seen Kirinyaga," he replied. "I have not yet seen Utopia."

"That is because you do not know how to look for it."

"You are a clever old man, Koriba, full of clever answers," said Sambeke, taking no offense. "Why have you not made yourself king of this entire planetoid?"

"The *mundumugu* is the repository of our traditions. That is all the power he seeks or needs."

"You could at least have had them build you a

house, instead of living like this. No Maasai lives in a *manyatta* any longer."

"And after the house would come a car?" I asked.

"Once you built some roads," he agreed.

"And then a factory to build more cars, and another one to build more houses, and then an impressive building for our Parliament, and perhaps a railroad line?" I shook my head. "That is a description of Kenya, not of Utopia."

"You are making a mistake," said Sambeke. "On my way here from the landing field—what is it called?"

"Haven."

"On my way here from Haven, I saw buffalo and kudu and impala. A hunting lodge by the river overlooking the plains would bring in a lot of tourist money."

"We do not hunt our grasseaters."

"You wouldn't have to," he said meaningfully. "And think of how much their money could help your people."

"May Ngai preserve us from people who want to help us," I said devoutly.

"You are a stubborn old man," he said. "I think I had better go talk to Koinnage. Which *shamba* is his?"

"The largest," I answered. "He is the paramount chief."

He nodded. "Of course. I will see you later, old man."

I nodded. "Yes, you will."

"And after I have killed your hyenas, perhaps we will share a gourd of *pombe* and discuss ways to turn this world into a Utopia. I have been very disappointed thus far."

So saying, he turned toward the village and began walking down the long, winding trail to Koinnage's *boma*.

He turned Koinnage's head, as I knew he would. By the time I had eaten and made my way to the village, the two of them were sitting beside a fire in front of the paramount chief's *boma*, and Sambeke was describing the hunting lodge he wanted to build by the river.

"*Jambo*, Koriba," said Koinnage, looking up at me as I approached them.

"*Jambo*, Koinnage," I responded, squatting down next to him.

"You have met William Sambeke?"

"I have met Sambeke," I said, and the Maasai grinned at my refusal to use his European name.

"He has many plans for Kirinyaga," continued Koinnage, as some of the villagers began wandering over.

"How interesting," I replied. "You asked for a hunter, and they have sent you a planner instead."

"Some of us," interjected Sambeke, an amused expression on his face, "have more than one talent."

"Some of us," I said, "have been here for half a day and have not yet begun to hunt."

"I will kill the hyenas tomorrow," said Sambeke, "when their bellies are full and they are too content to race away at my approach."

"How will you kill them?" I asked.

He carefully unlocked his gun case and pulled out his rifle, which was equipped with a telescopic sight.

Most of the villagers had never seen such a weapon, and they crowded around it, whispering to each other.

"Would you care to examine it?" he asked me.

I shook my head. "The weapons of the Europeans hold no interest for me."

"This rifle was manufactured in Zimbabwe, by members of the Shona tribe," he corrected me.

I shrugged. "Then they are black Europeans."

"Whatever they are, they make a splendid weapon," said Sambeke.

"For those who are afraid to hunt in the traditional way," I said.

"Do not taunt me, old man," said Sambeke, and suddenly a hush fell over the onlookers, for no man speaks thus to the *mundumugu*.

"I do not taunt you, Maasai," I said. "I merely point out why you have brought the weapon. It is no crime to be afraid of *fisi*."

"I fear nothing," he said heatedly.

"That is not true," I said. "Like all of us, you fear failure."

"I shall not fail with *this*," he said, patting the rifle.

"By the way," I asked, "was it not the Maasai who once proved their manhood by facing the lion armed only with a spear?"

"It was," he answered. "And it was the Maasai *and* the Kikuyu who lost most of their babies at birth, and who succumbed to every disease that passed through their villages, and who lived in shelters that could protect them from neither the rain nor the cold nor even the flesh-eaters of the veldt. It was the Maasai and the Kikuyu who learned from the Europeans, and who took back their land from the white men, and who built great cities where once there was only dust and swamps. Or, rather," he added, "it was the Maasai and *most* of the Kikuyu."

"I remember seeing a circus when I was in England," I said, raising my voice so that all could hear me, though I directed my remarks at Sambeke. "In it there was a chimpanzee. He was a very bright animal. They dressed him in human clothing, and he rode a human bicycle, and he played human music on a human flute—but that did not make him a human. In fact, he amused the humans because he was such a grotesque mockery of them ... just as the Maasai and Kikuyu who wear suits and drive cars and work in large buildings are not Europeans, but are instead a mockery of them."

"That is just your opinion, old man," said the Maasai, "and it is wrong."

"Is it?" I asked. "The chimpanzee had been tainted by his association with humans, so that he could never survive in the wild. And *you*, I notice, must have the Europeans' weapon to hunt an animal that your grandfathers would have gone out and slain with a knife or a spear."

"Are you challenging me, old man?" asked Sambeke, once again amused.

"I am merely pointing out why you have brought your rifle with you," I answered.

"No," he said. "You are trying to regain the power you lost when your people sent for me. But you have made a mistake."

"In what way?"

"You have made me your enemy."

"Will you shoot me with your rifle, then?" I asked calmly, for I knew he would not.

He leaned over and whispered to me, so that only I could hear him.

"We could have made a fortune together, old man. I would have been happy to share it with you, in exchange for you keeping your people in line, for a safari company will need many workers. But now you have publicly opposed me, and I cannot permit that."

"We must learn to live with disappointments," I said.

"I am glad you feel that way," he said. "For I plan to turn this world into a Utopia, rather than some Kikuyu dreamland."

Then, suddenly, he stood up.

"Boy," he said to Ndemi, who was standing at the outskirts of the crowd. "Bring me a spear."

Ndemi looked to me, and I nodded, for I could not believe that the Maasai would kill me with *any* weapon.

Ndemi brought the spear to Sambeke, who took it from him and leaned it against Koinnage's hut. Then he stood before the fire and slowly began removing all his clothes. When he was naked, with the firelight playing off his lean, hard body, looking like an African god, he picked up the spear and held it over his head.

"I go to hunt *fisi* in the dark, in the old way," he announced to the assembled villagers. "Your *mundumugu* has laid down the challenge, and if you are to listen to my counsel in the future, as I hope you will, you must know that I can meet any challenge he sets for me."

And before anyone could say a word or move to stop him, he strode boldly off into the night.

"Now he will die, and Maintenance will want to revoke our charter!" complained Koinnage.

"If he dies, it was his own decision, and Maintenance will not punish us in any way," I replied. I stared long and hard at him. "I wonder that you care."

"That I care if he should die?"

"That you care if Maintenance should revoke our charter," I answered. "If you listen to the Maasai, you will turn Kirinyaga into another Kenya, so why should you mind returning to the original Kenya?"

"He does not want to turn Kirinyaga into Kenya, but into Utopia," said Koinnage sullenly.

"We are already attempting to do that," I noted. "Does *his* Utopia include a big European house for the paramount chief?"

"We did not discuss it thoroughly," said Koinnage uneasily.

"And perhaps some extra cattle, in exchange for supplying him with porters and gunbearers?"

"He has good ideas," said Koinnage, ignoring my question. "Why should we carry our water from the river when he can create pumps and pipes to carry it for us?"

"Because if water is easy to obtain, it will become easy to waste, and we have no more water to waste here than we had in Kenya, where all the lakes have dried up because of far-seeing men like Sambeke."

"You have answers for everything," said Koinnage bitterly.

"No," I said. "But I have answers for this Maasai, for his questions have been asked many times before, and always in the past the Kikuyu have given the wrong answer."

Suddenly we heard a hideous scream from perhaps half a mile away.

"It is finished," said Koinnage grimly. "The Maasai is dead, and now we must answer to Maintenance."

"It did not sound like a man," said Ndemi.

"You are just a *mtoto*—a child," said Koinnage. "What do you know?"

"I know what Juma sounded like when *fisi* killed him," said Ndemi defiantly. "That is what I know."

We waited in silence to see if there would be another sound, but none was forthcoming.

"Perhaps it is just as well that *fisi* has killed the Maasai," said old Njobe at last. "I saw the building that he drew in the dirt, the one he would make for visitors, and it was an evil building. It was not round and safe from demons like our own huts, but instead it had corners, and everyone knows that demons live in corners."

"Truly, there would be a curse upon it," agreed another of the elders.

"What can one expect from one who hunts *fisi* at night?" added another.

"One can expect a dead *fisi*!" said Sambeke triumphantly, as he stepped out of the shadows and threw the bloody corpse of a large male hyena onto the ground. Everyone backed away from him in awe, and he turned to me, the firelight flickering off his sleek black body. "What do you say now, old man?"

"I say that you are a greater killer than *fisi*," I answered.

He smiled with satisfaction.

31

"Now," he said, "let us see what we can learn from this particular *fisi*." He turned to a young man. "Boy, bring a knife."

"His name is Kamabi," I said.

"I have not had time to learn names," replied Sambeke. He turned back to Kamabi. "Do as I ask, boy."

"He is a man," I said.

"It is difficult to tell in the dark," said Sambeke with a shrug.

Kamabi returned a moment later with an ancient hunting knife; it was so old and so rusty that Sambeke did not care to touch it, and so he merely pointed to the hyena.

"Kata hi ya tumbo," he said. "Slit the stomach here."

Kamabi knelt down and slit open the hyena's belly. The smell was terrible, but the Maasai picked up a stick and began prodding through the contents. Finally he stood up.

"I had hoped that we would find a bracelet or an earring," he said. "But it has been a long time since the boy was killed, and such things would have passed through *fisi* days ago."

"Koriba can roll the bones and tell if this is the one who killed Juma," said Koinnage.

Sambeke snorted contemptuously. "Koriba can roll the bones from now until the long rains come, but they will tell him nothing." He looked at the assembled villagers. "I have killed *fisi* in the old way to prove that I am no coward or European, to hunt only in the daylight and hide behind my gun. But now that I have shown you that I can do it, tomorrow I shall show you how many *fisi* I can kill in *my* way, and then you may decide which way is better,

Koriba's or mine." He paused. "Now I need a hut to sleep in, so that I may be strong and alert when the sun rises."

Every villager except Koinnage immediately volunteered his hut. The Maasai looked at each man in turn, and then turned to the paramount chief. "I will take yours," he said.

"But—" began Koinnage.

"And one of your wives to keep me warm in the night." He stared directly into Koinnage's eyes. "Or would you deny me your hospitality after I have killed *fisi* for you?"

"No," said Koinnage at last. "I will not deny you."

The Maasai shot me a triumphant smile. "It is still not Utopia," he said. "But it is getting closer."

The next morning Sambeke went out with his rifle.

I walked down to the village in the morning to give Zindu ointment to help dry up her milk, for her baby had been stillborn. When I was finished, I went through the *shambas*, blessing the scarecrows, and before long I had my usual large group of children beside me, begging me to tell them a story.

Finally, when the sun was high in the sky and it was too hot to keep walking, I sat down beneath the shade of an acacia tree.

"All right," I said. "Now you may have your story."

"What story will you tell us today, Koriba?" asked one of the girls.

"I think I shall tell you the tale of the Unwise Elephant," I said.

"Why was he unwise?" asked a boy.

"Listen, and you shall know," I said, and they all fell silent.

"Once there was a young elephant," I began, "and because he was young, he had not yet acquired the wisdom of his race. And one day this elephant chanced upon a city in the middle of the savannah, and he entered it, and beheld its wonders, and thought it was quite the most marvelous thing he had ever seen. All his life he had labored day and night to fill his belly, and here, in the city, were wonderful machines that could make his life so much easier that he was determined to own some of them.

"But when he approached the owner of a digging stick, with which he could find buried acacia pods, the owner said, 'I am a poor man, and I cannot give my digging stick to you. But because you want it so badly, I will make a trade.'

" 'But I have nothing to trade,' said the elephant unhappily.

" 'Of course you do,' said the man. 'If you will let me have your ivory, so that I can carve designs on it, you may have the digging stick.'

"The elephant considered this offer, and finally agreed, for if he had a digging stick he would no longer need his tusks to root up the ground.

"And he walked a little farther, and he came to an old woman with a weaving loom, and he thought this was a wonderful thing, for with it he would be able to make a blanket for himself so that he could stay warm during the long nights.

"He asked the woman for her weaving loom, and she replied that she would not give it away, but that she would be happy to trade it.

" 'All I have to trade is my digging stick,' said the elephant.

" 'But I do not need a digging stick,' said the old

woman. 'You must let me cut off one of your feet, that I may make a stool of it.'

"The elephant thought for a long time, and he remembered how cold he had been the previous night, and finally he agreed, and the trade was made.

"Then he came to a man who had a net, and the elephant thought that the net would be a wonderful thing to have, for now he could catch the fruits when he shook a tree, rather than having to hunt for them on the ground.

" 'I will not give you the net, for it took me many days to make it,' said the man, 'but I will trade it to you for your ears, which will make excellent sleeping mats.'

"Again the elephant agreed and finally he went back to the herd to show them the wonders he had brought from the city of men.

" 'What need have we for digging sticks?' asked his brother. 'No digging stick will last as long as our tusks.'

" 'It might be nice to have a blanket,' said his mother, 'but to make a blanket with a weaving loom we would need fingers, which we do not have.'

" 'I cannot see the purpose of a net for catching fruit from the trees,' said his father. 'For if you hold the net in your trunk, how will you shake the fruits loose from the tree, and if you shake the tree, how will you hold the net?'

" 'I see now that the tools of men are of no use to elephants,' said the young elephant. 'I can never be a man, so I will go back to being an elephant.'

"His father shook his head sadly. 'It is true that you are not a man—but because you have dealt with men, you are no longer an elephant either. You have lost your foot, and cannot keep up with the herd. You have given away your ivory, and you cannot dig for water, or churn up the ground to look for acacia pods. You have parted with your ears, and now you cannot flap them to cool your blood when the sun is high in the sky.'

"And so the elephant spent the rest of his unhappy life halfway between the city and the herd, for he could not become part of one and he was no longer part of the other."

I stopped, and stared off into the distance, where a small herd of impala was grazing just beyond one of our cultivated fields.

"Is that all?" asked the girl who had first requested the story.

"That is all," I said.

"It was not a very good story," she continued.

"Oh?" I asked, slapping a small insect that was crawling up my arm. "Why not?"

"Because the ending was not happy."

"Not all stories have happy endings," I said.

"I do not like unhappy endings," she said.

"Neither do I," I agreed. I paused and looked at her. "How do *you* think the story should end?"

"The elephant should not trade the things that make him an elephant, since he can never become a man."

"Very good," I said. "Would you trade the things that make you a Kikuyu, to try to be something you can never become?"

"Never!"

"Would any of you?" I asked my entire audience.

"No!" they cried.

"What if the elephant offered you his tusks, or the hyena offered you his fangs?"

"Never!"

I paused for just a moment before asking my next question.

"What if the Maasai offered you his gun?"

Most of the children yelled "No!", but I noticed that two of the older boys did not answer. I questioned them about it.

"A gun is not like tusks or teeth," said the taller of the two boys. "It is a weapon that men use."

"That is right," said the smaller boy, shuffling his bare feet in the dirt and raising a small cloud of dust. "The Maasai is not an animal. He is like us."

"He is not an animal," I agreed, "but he is not like us. Do the Kikuyu use guns, or live in brick houses, or wear European clothes?"

"No," said the boys in unison.

"Then if you were to use a gun, or live in a brick house, or wear European clothes, would you be a true Kikuyu?"

"No," they admitted.

"But would using a gun, or living in a brick house, or wearing European clothes, make you a Maasai or a European?"

"No."

"Do you see, then, why we must reject the tools and the gifts of outsiders? We can never become like them, but we can stop being Kikuyu, and if we stop being Kikuyu without becoming something else, then we are nothing."

"I understand, Koriba," said the taller boy.

"Are you sure?" I asked.

He nodded. "I am sure."

"Why are all your stories like this?" asked a girl.

"Like what?"

"They all have titles like the Unwise Elephant, or the Jackal and the Honeybird, or the Leopard and the Shrike, but when you explain them they are always about the Kikuyu."

"That is because I am a Kikuyu and you are a Kikuyu," I replied with a smile. "If we were leopards, then all my stories would really be about leopards."

I spent a few more minutes with them beneath the shade of the tree, and then I saw Ndemi approaching through the tall grass, his face alive with excitement.

"Well?" I said when he had joined us.

"The Maasai has returned," he announced.

"Did he kill any *fisi*?" I asked.

"*Mingi sana*," replied Ndemi. "Very many."

"Where is he now?"

"By the river with some of the young men who served as his gunbearers and skinners."

"I think I shall go visit them," I said, getting carefully to my feet, for my legs tend to get stiff when I sit in one position for too long. "Ndemi, you will come with me. The rest of you children are to go back to your *shambas*, and to think about the story of the Unwise Elephant."

Ndemi's chest puffed up like one of my roosters when I singled him out to accompany me, and a moment later we were walking across the sprawling savannah.

"What is the Maasai doing at the river?" I asked.

"He has cut down some young saplings with a *panga*," answered Ndemi, "and he is instructing some of the men to build something, but I do not know what it is."

I peered through the haze of heat and dust, and saw a small party of men approaching us.

"*I* know what it is," I said softly, for although I had never seen a sedan chair, I knew what one looked like, and it was currently approaching us as four Kikuyu bore the weight of the chair—and the Maasai—upon their sweating shoulders.

Since they were heading in our direction, I told Ndemi to stop walking, and we stood and waited for them.

"*Jambo*, old man!" said the Maasai when we were within earshot. "I have killed seven more hyenas this morning."

"*Jambo*, Sambeke," I replied. "You look very comfortable."

"It could use cushions," he said. "And the bearers do not carry it levelly. But I will make do with it."

"Poor man," I said, "who lacks cushions and thoughtful bearers. How did these oversights come to pass?"

"That is because it is not Utopia yet," he replied with a smile. "But it is getting very close."

"You will be sure to tell me when it arrives," I said.

"You will know, old man."

Then he directed his bearers to carry him to the village. Ndemi and I remained where we were, and watched him disappear in the distance.

That night there was a feast in the village to celebrate the slaying of the eight hyenas. Koinnage himself had slaughtered an ox, and there was much *pombe*, and the people were singing and dancing when I arrived, re-enacting the stalking and killing of the animals by their new savior.

The Maasai himself was seated on a tall chair, taller even than Koinnage's throne. In one hand he held a gourd of *pombe*, and the leather case that held his rifle was laid carefully across his lap. He was clad now in the red robe of his people, his hair was neatly braided in his tribal fashion, and his lean body glistened with oils that had been rubbed onto it. Two young girls, scarcely past circumcision age, stood behind him, hanging upon his every word.

"*Jambo*, old man!" he greeted me as I approached him.

"*Jambo*, Sambeke," I said.

"That is no longer my name," he said.

"Oh? And have you taken a Kikuyu name instead?"

"I have taken a name that the Kikuyu will understand," he replied. "It is what the village will call me from this day forth."

"You are not leaving, now that the hunt is over?"

He shook his head. "I am not leaving."

"You are making a mistake," I said.

"Not as big a mistake as you made when you chose not to be my ally," he responded. Then, after a brief pause, he smiled and added: "Do you not wish to know my new name?"

"I suppose I should know it, if you are to remain here for any length of time," I agreed.

He leaned over and whispered the word to me that Ngai had whispered to Gikuyu on the holy mountain millions of years earlier.

"Bwana?" I repeated.

He looked smugly at me, and smiled again.
"Now," he said, "it is Utopia."

Bwana spent the next few weeks making Kirinyaga a Utopia—for Bwana.

He took three young wives for himself, and he had
the villagers build him a large house by the river, a
house with windows and corners and verandas such
as the colonial Europeans might have built in Kenya
two centuries earlier.

He went hunting every day, collecting trophies for
himself and providing the village with more meat
than they had ever had before. At nights he went to
the village to eat and drink and dance, and then,
armed with his rifle, he walked through the darkness
to his own house.

Soon Koinnage was making plans to build a house
similar to Bwana's, right in the village, and many of
the young men wanted the Maasai to procure rifles for
them. This he refused to do, explaining that there could
be only one Bwana on Kirinyaga, and it was their job
to serve as trackers and cooks and skinners.

He no longer wore European clothes, but always
appeared in traditional Maasai dress, his hair metic-
ulously pleated and braided, his body bright and
glistening from the oils that his wives rubbed on him
each night.

I kept my own counsel and continued my duties,
caring for the sick, bringing the rains, reading the
entrails of goats, blessing the scarecrows, alleviating
curses. But I did not say another word to Bwana,
nor did he speak to me.

Ndemi spent more and more time with me, tend-
ing my goats and chickens, and even keeping my

boma clean, which is woman's work but which he volunteered to do.

Finally one day he approached me while I sat in the shade, watching the cattle grazing in a nearby field.

"May I speak, *mundumugu*?" he asked, squatting down next to me.

"You may speak, Ndemi," I answered.

"The Maasai has taken another wife," he said. "And he killed Karanja's dog because its barking annoyed him." He paused. "And he calls everyone 'Boy,' even the elders, which seems to me to be a term of disrespect."

"I know these things," I said.

"Why do you not do something, then?" asked Ndemi. "Are you not all-powerful?"

"Only Ngai is all-powerful," I said. "I am just the *mundumugu*."

"But is not the *mundumugu* more powerful than a Maasai?"

"Most of the people in the village do not seem to think so," I said.

"Ah!" he said. "You are angry with them for losing faith in you, and *that* is why you have not turned him into an insect and stepped on him."

"I am not angry," I said. "Merely disappointed."

"When will you kill him?" asked Ndemi.

"It would do no good to kill him," I replied.

"Why not?"

"Because they believe in his power, and if he died, they would just send for another hunter, who would become another Bwana."

"Then will you do nothing?"

"I will do something," I answered. "But killing

Bwana is not the answer. He must be humiliated before the people, so that they can see for themselves
that he is not, after all, a *mundumugu* who must be
listened to and obeyed."

"How will you do this?" asked Ndemi anxiously.

"I do not know yet," I said. "I must study him
further."

"I thought you knew everything already."

I smiled. "The *mundumugu* does not know everything, nor does he have to."

"Oh?"

"He must merely know more than his people."

"But you already know more than Koinnage and
the others."

"I must be sure I know more than the Maasai before I act," I said. "You may know how large the
leopard is, and how strong, and how fast, and how
cunning—but until you have studied him further,
and learned how he charges, and which side he fa-
vors, and how he tests the wind, and how he signals
an attack by moving his tail, you are at a disadvan-
tage if you hunt him. I am an old man, and I cannot
defeat the Maasai in hand-to-hand combat, so I must
study him and discover his weakness."

"And what if he has none?"

"Everything has a weakness."

"Even though he is stronger than you?"

"The elephant is the strongest beast of all, and yet
a handful of tiny ants inside his trunk can drive him
mad with pain to the point where he will kill himself." I paused. "You do not have to be stronger than
your opponent, for surely the ant is not stronger than
the elephant. But the ant knows the elephant's weakness, and I must learn the Maasai's."

He placed his hand to his chest.

"*I* believe in you, Koriba," he said.

"I am glad," I said, shielding my eyes as a hot breeze blew a cloud of dust across my hill. "For you alone will not be disappointed when I finally confront the Maasai."

"Will you forgive the men of the village?" he asked.

I paused before answering. "When they remember once more why we came to Kirinyaga, I will forgive them," I said at last.

"And if they do not remember?"

"I must make them remember," I said. I looked out across the savannah, following its contours as it led up the river and the woods. "Ngai has given the Kikuyu a second chance at Utopia, and we must not squander it."

"You and Koinnage, and even the Maasai, keep using that word, but I do not understand it."

"Utopia?" I asked.

He nodded. "What does it mean?"

"It means many things to many people," I replied. "To the true Kikuyu, it means to live as one with the land, to respect the ancient laws and rituals, and to please Ngai."

"That seems simple enough."

"It does, doesn't it?" I agreed. "And yet you cannot begin to imagine how many millions of men have died because their definition of Utopia differed from their neighbor's."

He stared at me. "Truly?"

"Truly. Take the Maasai, for example. His Utopia is to ride upon his sedan chair, and to shoot animals, and to take many wives, and to live in a big house by the river."

"It does not sound like a bad thing," observed Ndemi thoughtfully.

"It is not a bad thing—for the Maasai." I paused briefly. "But do you suppose it is Utopia for the men who must carry the chair, or the animals that he kills, or the young men of the village who cannot marry, or the Kikuyu who must build his house by the river?"

"I see," said Ndemi, his eyes widening. "Kirinyaga must be a Utopia for all of us, or it cannot be a Utopia at all." He brushed an insect from his cheek and looked at me. "Is that correct, Koriba?"

"You learn quickly, Ndemi," I said, reaching a hand out and rubbing the hair atop his head. "Perhaps some day you yourself will become a *mundumugu.*"

"Will I learn magic then?"

"You must learn many things to be a *mundumugu,*" I said. "Magic is the least of them."

"But it is the most impressive," he said. "It is what makes the people fear you, and fearing you, they are willing to listen to your wisdom."

As I considered his words, I finally began to get an inkling of how I would defeat Bwana and return my people to the Utopian existence that we had envisioned when we accepted our charter for Kirinyaga.

"Sheep!" growled Bwana. "All sheep! No wonder the Maasai preyed on the Kikuyu in the old days."

I had decided to enter the village at night, to further observe my enemy. He had drunk much *pombe,* and finally stripped off his red cloak and stood naked before Koinnage's *boma,* challenging the young men of the village to wrestle him. They stood back in the shadows, shaking like women, in awe of his physical prowess.

"I will fight three of you at once!" he said, looking around for any volunteers. There were none, and he threw back his head and laughed heartily.

"And you wonder why I am Bwana and you are a bunch of boys!"

Suddenly his eyes fell on me.

"*There* is a man who is not afraid of me," he announced.

"That is true," I said.

"Will *you* wrestle me, old man?"

I shook my head. "No, I will not."

"I guess you are just another coward."

"I do not fear the buffalo or the hyena, but I do not wrestle with *them*, either," I said. "There is a difference between courage and foolishness. You are a young man; I am an old one."

"What brings you to the village at night?" he asked. "Have you been speaking to your gods, plotting ways to kill me?"

"There is only one god," I replied, "and He disapproves of killing."

He nodded, an amused smile on his face. "Yes, it stands to reason that the god of sheep would disapprove of killing." Suddenly the smile vanished, and he stared contemptuously at me. "En-kai spits upon your god, old man."

"You call Him En-kai and we call Him Ngai," I said calmly, "but it is the same god, and the day will come when we all must answer to Him. I hope you will be as bold and fearless then as you are now."

"I hope your Ngai will not tremble before *me*," he retorted, posturing before his wives, who giggled at his arrogance. "Did I not go naked into the night, armed with only a spear, and slay *fisis*? Have I not killed more than one hundred beasts in less than thirty days? Your Ngai had better not test my temper."

"He will test more than your temper," I replied.

"What does *that* mean?"

"It means whatever you wish it to mean," I said. "I am old and tired, and I wish to sit by the fire and drink *pombe*."

With that I turned my back on him and walked over to Njobe, who was warming his ancient bones by a small fire just outside Koinnage's *boma*.

Unable to find an opponent with which to wrestle, Bwana drank more *pombe* and finally turned to his wives.

"No one will fight me," he said with mock misery. "And yet my fighting blood is boiling within my veins. Set me a task—any task—that I may do for your pleasure."

The three girls whispered together and giggled again, and finally one of them stepped forward, urged by the other two.

"We have seen Koriba place his hand in the fire without being burned," she said. "Can you do that?"

He snorted contemptuously. "A magician's trick, nothing more. Set me a true task."

"Set him an *easier* task," I said. "Obviously the fire is too painful."

He turned and glared at me. "What kind of lotion did you place on your hand before putting it in the fire, old man?" he asked in English.

I smiled at him. "That would be an *illusionist's* trick, not a magician's," I answered.

"You think to humiliate me before my people?" he said. "Think again, old man."

He walked to the fire, stood between Njobe and myself, and thrust his hand into it. His face was totally impassive, but I could smell the burning flesh. Finally he withdrew it and held it up.

"There is no magic to it!" he shouted in Swahili.

"But you are burned, my husband," said the wife who had challenged him.

"Did I cry out?" he demanded. "Did I cringe from pain?"

"No, you did not."

"Can any other man place his hand in the fire without crying out?"

"No, my husband."

"Who, then, is the greater man—Koriba, who protects himself with magic, or I, who need no magic to place my hand in the fire?"

"Bwana," said his wives in unison.

He turned to me and grinned triumphantly.

"You have lost again, old man."

But I had not lost.

I had gone to the village to study my enemy, and I had learned much from my visit. Just as a Kikuyu cannot become a Maasai, this Maasai could not become a Kikuyu. There was an arrogance that had been bred into him, an arrogance so great that it had not only elevated him to his current high status, but would prove to be his downfall as well.

The next morning Koinnage himself came to my *boma*.

"*Jambo*," I greeted him.

"*Jambo*, Koriba," he replied. "We must talk."

"About what?"

"About Bwana," said Koinnage.

"What about him?"

"He has overstepped himself," said Koinnage. "Last night, after you left, he decided that he had drunk too much *pombe* to return home, and he threw me out of my own hut—*me*, the paramount chief!" He paused to kick at a small lizard that had been approaching his foot, and then continued. "Not only that, but this morning he announced that he was taking my youngest wife, Kibo, for his own!"

"Interesting," I remarked, watching the tiny lizard as it scurried under a bush, then turned and stared at us.

"Is that all you can say?" he demanded. "I paid twenty cows and five goats for her. When I told him that, do you know what he did?"

"What?"

Koinnage held up a small silver coin for me to see. "He gave me a *shilling* from Kenya!" He spat upon the coin and threw it onto the dry, rocky slope beyond my *boma*. "And now he says that whenever he stays in the village he will sleep in my hut, and that I must sleep elsewhere."

"I am very sorry," I said. "But I warned you against sending for a hunter. It is his nature to prey upon all things: the hyena, the kudu, even the Kikuyu." I paused, enjoying his discomfort. "Perhaps you should tell him to go away."

"He would not listen."

I nodded. "The lion may sleep with the goat, and he may feed upon him, but he very rarely listens to him."

"Koriba, we were wrong," said Koinnage, his face

a mask of desperation. "Can you not rid us of this intruder?"

"Why?" I asked.

"I have already told you."

I shook my head slowly. "You have told me why *you* have cause to resent him," I answered. "That is not enough."

"What more must I say?" asked Koinnage.

I paused and looked at him. "It will come to you in the fullness of time."

"Perhaps we can contact Maintenance," suggested Koinnage. "Surely *they* have the power to make him leave."

I sighed deeply. "Have you learned nothing?"

"I do not understand."

"You sent for the Maasai because he was stronger than *fisi*. Now you want to send for Maintenance because they are stronger than the Maasai. If one man can so change our society, what do you think will happen when we invite many men? Already our young men talk of hunting instead of farming, and wish to build European houses with corners where demons can hide, and beg the Maasai to supply them with guns. What will they want when they have seen all the wonders that Maintenance possesses?"

"Then how are we to rid ourselves of the Maasai?"

"When the time comes, he will leave," I said.

"You are certain?"

"I am the *mundumugu*."

"When will this time be?" asked Koinnage.

"When you know *why* he must leave," I answered. "Now perhaps you should return to the village, lest you discover that he wants your other wives as well."

Panic spread across Koinnage's face, and he raced

back down the winding trail to the village without another word.

I spent the next few days gathering bark from some of the trees at the edge of the savannah, and when I had gathered as much as I needed I added certain herbs and roots and mashed them to a pulp in an old turtle shell. I added some water, placed it in a cooking gourd, and began simmering the concoction over a small fire.

When I was done I sent for Ndemi, who arrived about half an hour later.

"*Jambo*, Koriba," he said.

"*Jambo*, Ndemi," I replied.

He looked at my cooking gourd and wrinkled his nose. "What is that?" he asked. "It smells terrible."

"It is not for eating," I replied.

"I hope not," he said devoutly.

"Be careful not to touch it," I said, walking over to the tree that grew within my *boma* and sitting down in its shade. Ndemi, giving the gourd a wide berth, joined me.

"You sent for me," he said.

"Yes, I did."

"I am glad. The village is not a good place to be."

"Oh?"

He nodded. "A number of the young men now follow Bwana everywhere. They take goats from the *shambas* and cloth from the huts, and nobody dares to stop them. Kanjara tried yesterday, but the young men hit him and made his mouth bleed while Bwana watched and laughed."

I nodded, for none of this surprised me.

"I think it is almost time," I said, waving my hand

51

to scare away some flies that also sought shade beneath the tree and were buzzing about my face.

"Almost time for what?"

"For Bwana to leave Kirinyaga." I paused. "That is why I sent for you."

"The *mundumugu* wishes me to help him?" said Ndemi, his young face shining with pride.

I nodded.

"I will do anything you say," vowed Ndemi.

"Good. Do you know who makes the oils with which Bwana anoints himself?"

"Old Wambu makes them."

"You must bring me two gourds filled with them."

"I thought only the Maasai anoints himself," said Ndemi.

"Just do as I say. Now, have you a bow?"

"No, but my father does. He has not used it in many years, so he will not mind if I take it."

"I do not want anyone to know you have it."

Ndemi shrugged and idly drew a pattern in the dirt with his forefinger. "He will blame the young men who follow Bwana."

"And has your father any arrows with sharp tips?"

"No," said Ndemi. "But I can make some."

"I want you to make some this afternoon," I said. "Ten should be enough."

Ndemi drew an arrow in the dirt. "Like so?" he asked.

"A little shorter," I said.

"I can get the feathers for the arrows from the chickens in our *boma*," he suggested.

I nodded. "That is good."

"Do you want me to shoot an arrow into Bwana?"

"I told you once: the Kikuyu do not kill their fellow men."

"Then what do you want me to do with the arrows?"

"Bring them back here to my *boma* when you have made them," I said. "And bring ten pieces of cloth in which to wrap them."

"And then what?"

"And then we will dip them into the poison I have been making."

He frowned. "But you do not wish me to shoot an arrow into Bwana?" He paused. "What shall I shoot, then?"

"I will tell you when the time comes," I said. "Now return to the village and do what I have asked you to do."

"Yes, Koriba," he said, running out of my *boma* and down the hill on his strong young legs as a number of guinea fowl, squawking and screeching, moved resentfully out of his path.

It was less than an hour later that Koinnage once again climbed my hill, this time accompanied by Njobe and two other elders, all wearing their tribal robes.

"*Jambo*, Koriba," said Koinnage unhappily.

"*Jambo*," I replied.

"You told me to come back when I understood why Bwana must leave," said Koinnage. He spat on the ground, and a tiny spider raced away. "I have come."

"And what have you learned?" I asked, raising my hand to shade my eyes from the sun.

He lowered his eyes to the ground, uncomfortable as a child being questioned by his father.

"I have learned that a Utopia is a delicate thing

which requires protection from those who would force their will upon it."

"And you, Njobe?" I said. "What have you learned?"

"Our life here was very good," he answered. "And I believed that goodness was its own defense." He sighed deeply. "But it is not."

"Is Kirinyaga worth defending?" I asked.

"How can you, of all people, ask that?" demanded one of the other two elders.

"The Maasai can bring many machines and much money to Kirinyaga," I said. "He seeks only to improve us, not destroy us."

"It would not be Kirinyaga any longer," said Njobe. "It would be Kenya all over again."

"He has corrupted everything he has touched," said Koinnage, his face contorted with rage and humiliation. "My own son has become one of his followers. No longer does he show respect for his father, or for our women or our traditions. He speaks only of money and guns now, and he worships Bwana as if he were Ngai Himself." He paused. "You must help us, Koriba."

"Yes," added Njobe. "We were wrong not to listen to you."

I stared at each of their worried faces in turn, and finally I nodded.

"I will help you."

"When?"

"Soon."

"*How* soon?" persisted Koinnage, coughing as the wind blew a cloud of dust past his face. "We cannot wait much longer."

"Within a week the Maasai will be gone," I said.

"Within a week?" repeated Koinnage.

"That is my promise." I paused. "But if we are to purify our society, his followers may have to leave with him."

"You cannot take my son from me!" said Koinnage.

"The Maasai has already taken him," I pointed out. "I will have to decide if he will be allowed to return."

"But he is to be the paramount chief when I die."

"That is my price, Koinnage," I said firmly. "You must let me decide what to do with the Maasai's followers." I placed a hand to my heart. "I will make a just decision."

"I do not know," muttered Koinnage.

I shrugged. "Then live with the Maasai."

Koinnage stared intently at the ground, as if the ants and termites could tell him what to do. Finally he sighed.

"It will be as you say," he agreed unhappily.

"How will you rid us of the Maasai?" asked Njobe.

"I am the *mundumugu*," I answered noncommittally, for I wanted no hint of my plan to reach Bwana's ears.

"It will take powerful magic," said Njobe.

"Do you doubt my powers?" I asked.

Njobe would not meet my gaze. "No, but . . ."

"But what?"

"But he is like a god. He will be difficult to destroy."

"We have room for only one god," I said, "and His name is Ngai."

They returned to the village, and I went back to blending my poison.

* * *

While I waited for Ndemi to return, I took a thin piece of wood and carved a tiny hole in it. Then I took a long needle, stuck it lengthwise through the entire length of the wood, and withdrew it.

Finally I placed the wood to my lips and blew into the hole. I could hear no sound, but the cattle in the pasture suddenly raised their heads, and two of my goats began racing frantically in circles. I tried my makeshift whistle twice more, received the same reaction, and finally put it aside.

Ndemi arrived in midafternoon, carrying the oil gourds, his father's ancient bow and ten carefully-crafted arrows. He had been unable to find any metal, but he had carved very sharp points at the end of each. I checked the bowstring, decided that it still had resiliency, and nodded my approval.

Then, very carefully making sure not to let any of the poison come in contact with my flesh, I dipped the head of each arrow into my solution, and wrapped them in the ten pieces of cloth Ndemi had brought.

"It is good," I said. "Now we are ready."

"What must I do, Koriba?" he asked.

"In the old days when we still lived in Kenya, only Europeans were allowed to hunt, and they used to be paid to take other Europeans on safari," I explained. "It was important to these white hunters that their clients killed many animals, for if they were disappointed, they would either not return or would pay a different white hunter to take them on their next safari." I paused. "Because of this, the hunters would sometimes train a pride of lions to come out and be killed."

"How would they do this, Koriba?" asked Ndemi, his eyes wide with wonder.

"The white hunter would send his tracker out ahead of the safari," I said, pouring the oil into six smaller gourds as I spoke. "The tracker would go into the veldt where the lions lived, and kill a wildebeest or a zebra, and slit open its belly, so that the odors wafted in the wind. Then he would blow a whistle. The lions would come, either because of the odors or because they were curious about the strange new sound.

"The tracker would kill another zebra the next day, and blow the whistle again, and the lions would come again. This went on every day until the lions knew that when they heard the whistle, there would be a dead animal waiting for them—and when the tracker had finally trained them to come at the sound of the whistle, he would return to the safari, and lead the hunter and his clients to the veldt where the lions dwelt, and then blow the whistle. The lions would run toward the sound, and the hunter's clients would collect their trophies."

I smiled at his delighted reaction, and wondered if anyone left on Earth knew that the Kikuyu had anticipated Pavlov by more than a century.

Then I handed Ndemi the whistle I had carved.

"This is your whistle," I said. "You must not lose it."

"I will place a thong around my neck and tie it to the thong," he said. "I will not lose it."

"If you do," I continued, "I will surely die a terrible death."

"You can trust me, *mundumugu*."

"I know I can." I picked up the arrows and handed

57

them carefully to him. "These are yours," I said. "You must be very careful with them. If you cut your skin on them, or press them against a wound, you will almost certainly die, and not all of my powers will be able to save you."

"I understand," he said, taking the arrows gingerly and setting them on the ground next to his bow.

"Good," I said. "Do you know the forest that is half a mile from the house Bwana has built by the river?"

"Yes, Koriba."

"Each day I want you to go there and slay a grasseater with one of your poisoned arrows. Do not try to kill the buffalo, because he is too dangerous—but you may kill any other grasseater. Once it is dead, pour all the oil from one of these six gourds onto it."

"And then shall I blow the whistle for the hyenas?" he asked.

"Then you will climb a nearby tree, and only when you are safe in its branches are you to blow the whistle," I said. "They will come—slowly the first day, more rapidly the second and third, and almost instantly by the fourth. You will sit in the tree for a long time after they have eaten and gone, and then you will climb down and return to your *boma*."

"I will do as you ask, Koriba," he said. "But I do not see how this will make Bwana leave Kirinyaga."

"That is because you are not yet a *mundumugu*," I replied with a smile. "But I am not yet through instructing you."

"What else must I do?"

"I have one final task to set before you," I continued. "Just before sunrise on the seventh day, you will leave your *boma* and kill a seventh animal."

"I only have six gourds of oil," he pointed out.

"You will not need any on the seventh day. They will come simply because you whistle." I paused to make sure he was following my every word. "As I say, you will kill a grasseater before sunrise, but this time you will not spread oil on him, and you will not blow your whistle immediately. You will climb a tree that affords you a clear view of the plains between the woods and the river. At some point you will see me wave my hand *thus*—" I demonstrated a very definite rotating motion with my right hand "—and then you must blow the whistle *immediately*. Do you understand?"

"I understand."

"Good."

"And what you have told me to do will rid Kirinyaga of Bwana forever?" he asked.

"Yes."

"I wish I knew how," persisted Ndemi.

"This much I will tell you," I said. "Being a civilized man, he will expect two things: that I will confront him on my own territory, and that—because I, too, have been educated by the Europeans—that I will use the Europeans' technology to defeat him."

"But you will not do what he expects?"

"No," I said. "He still does not understand that our traditions supply us with everything we need on Kirinyaga. I will confront him on his own battleground, and I will defeat him with the weapons of the Kikuyu and not the Europeans." I paused again. "And now, Ndemi, you must go slay the first of the grasseaters, or it will be dark before you go home, and I do not want you walking across the savannah at night."

He nodded, picked up his whistle and his weapons, and strode off toward the woods by the river.

On the sixth night I walked down to the village, arriving just after dark.

The dancing hadn't started yet, though most of the adults had already gathered. Four young men, including Koinnage's son, tried to block my way, but Bwana was in a generous mood, and he waved them aside.

"Welcome, old man," he said, sitting atop his tall stool. "It has been many days since I have seen you."

"I have been busy."

"Plotting my downfall?" he asked with an amused smile.

"Your downfall was predetermined by Ngai," I replied.

"And what will cause my downfall?" he continued, signaling one of his wives—he had five now—to bring him a fresh gourd of *pombe*.

"The fact that you are not a Kikuyu."

"What is so special about the Kikuyu?" he demanded. "They are a tribe of sheep who stole their women from the Wakamba and their cattle and goats from the Luo. Their sacred mountain, from which this world took its name, they stole from the Maasai, for *Kirinyaga* is a Maasai word."

"Is that true, Koriba?" asked one of the younger men.

I nodded. "Yes, it is true. In the language of the Maasai, *kiri* means *mountain*, and *nyaga* means *light*. But while it is a Maasai word, it is the Kikuyu's Mountain of Light, given to us by Ngai."

"It is the Maasai's mountain," said Bwana. "Even its peaks are named after Maasai chieftains."

"There has never been a Maasai on the holy mountain," said old Njobe.

"We owned the mountain first, or it would bear a Kikuyu name," responded Bwana.

"Then the Kikuyu must have slain the Maasai, or driven them away," said Njobe with a sly smile.

This remark angered Bwana, for he threw his gourd of *pombe* at a passing goat, hitting it on the flanks with such power that it bowled the goat over. The animal quickly got to its feet and raced through the village, bleating in terror.

"You are fools!" growled Bwana. "And if indeed the Kikuyu drove the Maasai from the mountain, then I will now redress the balance. I now proclaim myself Laibon of Kirinyaga, and declare that it is no longer a Kikuyu world."

"What is a Laibon?" asked one of the men.

"It is the Maasai word for king," I said.

"How can this not be a Kikuyu world, when everyone except you is a Kikuyu?" Njobe demanded of Bwana.

Bwana pointed at his five young henchmen. "I hereby declare these men to be Maasai."

"You cannot make them Maasai just by calling them Maasai."

Bwana grinned as the flickering firelight cast strange patterns on his sleek, shining body. "I can do anything I want. I am the Laibon."

"Perhaps Koriba has something to say about that," said Koinnage, for he knew that the week was almost up.

61

Bwana stared at me belligerently. "Well, old man, do you dispute my right to be king?"

"No," I said. "I do not."

"Koriba!" exclaimed Koinnage.

"You cannot mean that!" said Njobe.

"We must be realistic," I said. "Is he not our mightiest hunter?"

Bwana snorted. "I am your *only* hunter."

I turned to Koinnage. "Who else but Bwana could walk naked into the veldt, armed only with a spear, and slay *fisi*?"

Bwana nodded his head. "That is true."

"Of course," I continued, "none of us saw him do it, but I am sure he would not lie to us."

"Do you dispute that I killed *fisi* with a spear?" demanded Bwana heatedly.

"I do not dispute it," I said earnestly. "I have no doubt that you could do it again whenever you wished."

"That is true, old man," he said, somewhat assuaged.

"In fact," I continued, "perhaps we should celebrate your becoming Laibon with another such hunt—but this time in the daylight, so that your subjects may see for themselves the prowess and courage of their king."

He took another gourd from his youngest wife and stared at me intently. "Why are you saying this, old man? What do you really want?"

"Only what I have said," I replied, spitting on my hands to show my sincerity.

He shook his head. "No," he said. "You are up to some mischief."

I shrugged. "Well, if you would rather not . . ."

"Perhaps he is afraid to," said Njobe.

"I fear nothing!" snapped Bwana.

"Certainly he does not fear *fisi*," I said. "That much should be evident by now."

"Right," said Bwana, still staring at me.

"Then if he does not fear *fisi*, what *does* he fear about a hunt?" asked Njobe.

"He does not wish to hunt because *I* suggested it," I replied. "He still does not trust me, and that is understandable."

"Why is that understandable?" demanded Bwana. "Do you think I fear your mumbo-jumbo like the other sheep do?"

"I have not said that," I answered.

"You have no magic, old man," he said, getting to his feet. "You have only tricks and threats, and these mean nothing to a Maasai." He paused, and then raised his voice so that everyone could hear him. "I will spend the night in Koinnage's hut, and then I will hunt *fisi* tomorrow morning, in the old way, so that all my subjects can see their Laibon in combat."

"Tomorrow morning?" I repeated.

He glared at me, his Maasai arrogance chiseled in every feature of his lean, handsome face.

"At sunrise."

I awoke early the next morning, as usual, but this time, instead of building a fire and sitting next to it until the chill had vanished from my aged bones, I donned my *kikoi* and walked immediately to the village. All of the men were gathered around Koinnage's *boma*, waiting for Bwana to emerge.

Finally he came out of his hut, his body anointed beneath his red cloak. He seemed clear-eyed despite the vast quantities of *pombe* he had imbibed the previous night, and in his right hand he clutched the same spear he had used during his very first hunt on Kirinyaga.

Contemptuous of us all, he looked neither right nor left, but began walking through the village and out onto the savannah toward the river. We fell into step behind him, and our little procession continued until we were perhaps a mile from his house. Then he stopped and held a hand up.

"You will come no farther," he announced, "or your numbers will frighten *fisi* away."

He let his red cloak fall to the ground and stood, naked and glistening, in the morning sunlight.

"Now watch, my sheep, and see how a true king hunts."

He hefted his spear once, to get the feel of it, and then he strode off into the waist-high grass.

Koinnage sidled up to me. "You promised that he would leave today," he whispered.

"So I did."

"He is still here."

"The day is not yet over."

"You're *sure* he will leave?" persisted Koinnage.

"Have I ever lied to my people?" I responded.

"No," he said, stepping back. "No, you have not."

We fell silent again, looking out across the plains. For a long time we could see nothing at all. Then Bwana emerged from a clump of bushes and walked boldly toward a spot about fifty yards ahead of him.

And then the wind shifted and suddenly the air was pierced by the ear-splitting laughter of hyenas as they caught scent of his oiled body. We could see grass swaying as the pack made their way toward Bwana, yelping and cackling as they approached.

For a moment he stood his ground, for he was truly a brave man, but then, when he saw their number and realized that he could kill no more than one of them, he hurled his spear at the nearest hyena and raced to a nearby acacia tree, clambering up it just before the first six hyenas reached its base.

Within another minute there were fifteen full-grown hyenas circling the tree, snarling and laughing at him, and Bwana had no choice but to remain where he was.

"How disappointing," I said at last. "I believed him when he said he was a mighty hunter."

"He is mightier than you, old man," said Koinnage's son.

"Nonsense," I said. "Those are just hyenas around his tree, not demons." I turned to Koinnage's son and his companions. "I thought you were his friends. Why do you not go to help him?"

They shifted uneasily, and then Koinnage's son spoke: "We are unarmed, as you can see."

"What difference does that make?" I said. "You are almost Maasai, and they are just hyenas."

"If they are so harmless, why don't *you* make them go away?" demanded Koinnage's son.

"This is not my hunt," I replied.

"You cannot make them go away, so do not chide us for standing here."

"I can make them go away," I said. "Am I not the *mundumugu*?"

"Then do so!" he challenged me.

I turned to the men of the village. "The son of

Koinnage has put a challenge to me. Do you wish me to save the Maasai?"

"No!" they said almost as one.

I turned to the young man. "There you have it."

"You are lucky, old man," he said, a sullen expression on his face. "You could not have done it."

"*You* are the lucky one," I said.

"Why?" he demanded.

"Because you called me old man, rather than *mundumugu* or *mzee*, and I have not punished you." I stared unblinking at him. "But know that should you ever call me old man again, I will turn you into the smallest of rodents and leave you in the field for the jackals to feed upon."

I uttered my statement with such conviction that he suddenly seemed less sure of himself.

"You are bluffing, *mundumugu*," he said at last. "You have no magic."

"You are a foolish young man," I said, "for you have seen my magic work in the past, and you know it will work again in the future."

"Then make the hyenas disperse," he said.

"If I do so, will you and your companions swear fealty to me, and respect the laws and traditions of the Kikuyu?"

He considered my proposition for a long moment, then nodded.

"And the rest of you?" I asked, turning to his companions.

There were mumbled assents.

"Very well," I said. "Your fathers and the village elders will bear witness to your agreement."

I began walking across the plain toward the tree where Bwana sat, glaring down at the hyenas. When

I got within perhaps three hundred yards of them they noticed me and began approaching, constantly testing the wind and growling hungrily.

"In the name of Ngai," I intoned, "the *mundu-mugu* orders you to begone!"

As I finished the sentence, I waved my right arm at them in just the way I had demonstrated to Ndemi.

I heard no whistle, for it was above the range of human hearing, but instantly the entire pack turned and raced off toward the woods.

I watched them for a moment, then turned back to my people.

"Now go back to the village," I said sternly. "I will tend to Bwana."

They retreated without a word, and I approached the tree from which Bwana had watched the entire pageant. He had climbed down and was waiting for me when I arrived.

"I have saved you with my magic," I said, "but now it is time for you to leave Kirinyaga."

"It was a trick!" he exclaimed. "It was not magic."

"Trick or magic," I said, "what difference does it make? It will happen again, and next time I will not save you."

"Why should I believe you?" he demanded sullenly.

"I have no reason to lie to you," I said. "The next time you go hunting they will attack again, so many *fisi* that even your European gun cannot kill them all, and I will not be here to save you." I paused. "Leave while you can, Maasai. They will not be back for half an hour. You have time to walk to Haven by then, and I will use my computer to tell Maintenance that you are waiting to be taken back to Earth."

He looked deep into my eyes. "You are telling the truth," he said at last.

"I am."

"How did you do it, old man?" he asked. "I deserve to know that much before I leave."

I paused for a long moment before answering him.

"I am the *mundumugu*," I replied at last, and, turning my back on him, I returned to the village.

We tore his house down that afternoon, and in the evening I called down the rains, which purified Kirinyaga of the last taint of the corruption that had been in our midst.

The next morning I walked down the long, winding path to the village to bless the scarecrows, and the moment I arrived I was surrounded by the children, who asked for a story.

"All right," I said, gathering them in the shade of an acacia tree. "Today I shall tell you the story of the Arrogant Hunter."

"Has it a happy ending?" asked one of the girls.

I looked around the village and saw my people contentedly going about their daily chores, then stared out across the tranquil green plains.

"Yes," I said. "This time it has."

BULLY!

I

The date was January 8, 1910.

"At midnight we had stopped at the station of Koba, where we were warmly received by the district commissioner, and where we met half a dozen of the professional elephant hunters, who for the most part make their money, at hazard of their lives, by poaching ivory in the Congo. They are a hard-bit set, these elephant poachers; there are few careers more adventurous, or fraught with more peril, or which make heavier demands upon the daring, the endurance, and the physical hardihood of those who follow them. Elephant hunters face death at every turn, from fever, from the assaults of warlike native tribes, from their conflicts with their giant

*quarry; and the unending strain on their health
and strength is tremendous."*

—Theodore Roosevelt
African Game Trails

"*. . . When we were all assembled in my tent
and champagne had been served out to everyone
except Roosevelt—who insisted on drinking non-
intoxicants, though his son Kermit joined us—
he raised his glass and gave the toast 'To the
Elephant Poachers of the Lado Enclave.' As we
drank with him one or two of us laughingly protested his bluntness, so he gravely amended his
toast to 'The Gentleman Adventurers of Central
Africa,' 'for,' he added, 'that is the title by which
you would have been known in Queen Eliza-
beth's time.'*

"*A real man, with the true outdoor spirit, the
ex-President's sympathy with and real envy of
the life we were leading grew visibly as the evening advanced; and he finally left us with evident reluctance. I, for one, was shaken by the
hand three times as he made for the door on
three separate occasions; but each time, after
hesitatingly listening to the beginning of some
new adventure by one of the boys, he again sat
down to hear another page from our every-day
life. We even urged him to chuck all his political
work and come out like the great white man he
was, and join us. If he would do this, we promised to put a force under his command to organize the hunting and pioneering business of
Central Africa, and perhaps make history. He*

*was, I believe, deeply moved by this offer; and
long afterwards he told a friend that no honor
ever paid him had impressed and tempted him
like that which he received from the poachers
of the Lado Enclave."*

—John Boyes
Company of Adventurers

Roosevelt walked to the door of the tent, then
paused and turned back to face Boyes.

"A force, you say?" he asked thoughtfully, as a
lion coughed and a pair of hyenas laughed mania-
cally in the distance.

"That's right, Mr. President," said Boyes, getting
to his feet. "I can promise you at least fifty men like
ourselves. They may not be much to look at, but
they'll be men who aren't afraid to work or to fight,
and each and every one of them will be loyal to you,
sir."

"Father, it's getting late," called Kermit from outside the tent.

"You go along," said Roosevelt distractedly. "I'll
join you in a few minutes." He turned back to Boyes.
"Fifty men?"

"That's right, Mr. President."

"Fifty men to tame the whole of Central Africa?"
mused Roosevelt.

Boyes nodded. "That's right. There's seven of us
right here; we could have the rest assembled inside
of two weeks."

"It's very tempting," admitted Roosevelt, trying to
suppress a guilty smile. "It would be a chance to be
both a boy and a President again."

"The Congo would make one hell of a private hunting preserve, sir," said Boyes.

The American was silent for a moment, and finally shook his massive head. "It couldn't be done," he said at last. "Not with fifty men."

"No," said Boyes. "I suppose not."

"There are no roads, no telephones, no telegraph lines." Roosevelt paused, staring at the flickering lanterns that illuminated the interior of the tent. "And the railway ends in Uganda."

"No access to the sea, either," agreed Boyes pleasantly, as the lion coughed again and a herd of hippos started bellowing in the nearby river.

"No," said Roosevelt with finality. "It simply couldn't be done—not with fifty men, not with five thousand."

Boyes grinned. "Not a chance in the world."

"A man would have to be mad to consider it," said Roosevelt.

"I suppose so, Mr. President," said Boyes.

Roosevelt nodded his head for emphasis. "Totally, absolutely mad."

"No question about it," said Boyes, still grinning at the burly American. "When do we start?"

"Tomorrow morning," said Roosevelt, his teeth flashing as he finally returned Boyes' grin. "By God, it'll be bully!"

II

"FATHER?"

Roosevelt, sitting on a chair in front of his tent, continued staring through his binoculars.

"Kermit, you're standing in front of a lilac-breasted roller and a pair of crowned cranes."

Kermit didn't move, and finally Roosevelt put his binoculars down on a nearby table. He pulled a notebook out of his pocket and began scribbling furiously.

"Remarkable bird viewing here," he said as he added the roller and the cranes to his list. "That's thirty-four species I've seen today, and we haven't even had breakfast yet." He looked up at his son. "I love these chilly Ugandan nights and mornings. They remind me of the Yellowstone. I trust you slept well?"

"Yes, I did."

"Wonderful climate," said Roosevelt. "Just wonderful!"

"Father, I'd like to speak to you for a few moments, if I may."

Roosevelt carefully tucked the notebook back into his breast pocket. "Certainly," he replied. "What would you like to talk about?"

Kermit looked around, found another canvas chair, carried it over next to his father, and sat down on it.

"This entire enterprise seems ill-conceived, Father."

Roosevelt seemed amused. "That's your considered opinion, is it?"

"One man can't civilize a country half the size of the United States," continued Kermit. "Not even you."

"Kermit, when I was twelve years old, the best doctors in the world told me I'd always be underweight and sickly," said Roosevelt. "But when I was nineteen, I was the lightweight boxing champion of Harvard."

"I know, Father."

"Don't interrupt. People told me I couldn't write a proper sentence, but I've written twenty books, and four of them have been best-sellers. They told me that politics was no place for a young man, but when I was twenty-four I was Speaker of the House of the New York State Legislature. They told me that law and order had no place in the West, but I went out and single-handedly captured three armed killers in the Dakota Bad Lands during the Winter of the Blue Snow." Roosevelt paused. "Even my Rough Riders said we couldn't take San Juan Hill; I took it." He stared at his son. "So don't tell me what I can't do, Kermit."

"But this isn't like anything else you've done," persisted Kermit.

"What better reason is there to do it?" said Roosevelt with a delighted grin.

"But—"

"Ex-Presidents are supposed to sit around in their rocking chairs and only come out for parades. Well, I'm fifty-one years old, and I'm not ready to retire yet. Another opportunity like this may never come along." Roosevelt gazed off to the west, toward the Congo. "Think of it, Kermit! More than half a million square miles, filled with nothing but animals and savages and a few missionaries. The British and French and Portuguese and Belgians and Italians all have had their chance at this continent; Africa ought to have one country developed by someone who will bring them American know-how and American democracy and American values. We're a rustic, frontier race ourselves; who better to civilize yet another frontier?" He paused, envisioning a future that was as clear to him as the present. "And think of the natural resources! We'll turn it into a protectorate, and give it favored nation trading status. There's lumber here to build thirty million houses, and where we've cleared the forests away we'll create farms and cities. It will be America all over again—only this time there will be no slavery, no genocide practiced against an indigenous people, no slaughter of the buffalo. I'll use America not as a blueprint, but as a first draft, and I'll learn from our past mistakes."

"But it *isn't* another America, Father," said Kermit. "It's a harsh, savage country, filled with hundreds of tribes whose only experience with white men is slavery."

"Then they'll be happy to find a white man who is willing to redress the balance, won't they?" replied Roosevelt with a confident smile.

"What about the legalities involved?" persisted Kermit. "The Congo is a Belgian colony."

"They've had their chance, and they've muddled it badly." Roosevelt paused. "Suppose you let *me* worry about the Belgians."

Kermit seemed about to argue the point, then realized the fruitlessness of further debate. "All right," he said with a sigh.

"Was there anything else?"

"Yes," said Kermit. "What do you know about this man Boyes?"

"The man's a true pioneer," said Roosevelt admiringly. "He should have been an American."

Kermit shook his head. "The man's a scalawag."

"That's your conclusion after being wined and dined in his tent for a single evening?"

"No, Father. But while you were taking your morning walk and watching birds, I was talking to some of his companions about him. They thought they were bragging about him, and telling me stories that would impress me—but what I heard gave me a true picture of the man."

"For example?" asked Roosevelt.

"He's always in trouble—with the law, with the British army, with the Colonial Office." Kermit paused. "They've tried to deport him from East Africa twice. Did you know that?"

"Certainly I know it," answered Roosevelt. Suddenly he grinned and pointed to a small book that was on the table next to his binoculars. "I spent most of the night reading his memoirs. Remarkable man!"

"Then you know that the British government arrested him for . . ." Kermit searched for the word.

"Dacoity?"

Kermit nodded. "Yes."

"Do you know what it means?" asked his father.

"No," admitted Kermit.

"In this particular case, it means that he signed a treaty with the Kikuyu and got them to open their land to white settlement, and some higher-up in the colonial government felt that Mr. Boyes was usurping his authority." Roosevelt chuckled. "So they sent a squad of six men into Kikuyuland to arrest him, and they found him surrounded by five thousand armed warriors. And since none of the arresting officers cared very much for the odds, Mr. Boyes volunteered to march all the way to Mombasa on his own recognizance." Roosevelt paused and grinned. "When he walked into court with his five thousand Kikuyu, the case was immediately thrown out." He laughed. "Now, that's a story that could have come out of our own Wild West."

"There were other stories, too, Father," said Kermit. "Less savory stories."

"Good," said Roosevelt. "Then he and I will have something to talk about on the way to the Congo."

"You know, of course, that he's the so-called White King of the Kikuyu."

"And I'm an honorary Indian chief. We have a lot in common."

"You have nothing in common," protested Kermit. "You *helped* our Indians. Boyes became king through deceit and treachery."

"He walked into a savage kingdom that had never permitted a white man to enter it before, and within two years he became the king of the entire Kikuyu nation. That's just the kind of man I need for the work at hand."

"But Father—"

"This is a harsh, savage land, Kermit, and I'm embarking on an enterprise that is for neither the timid nor the weak," said Roosevelt with finality. "He's the man I want."

"You're certain that you won't reconsider?"

Roosevelt shook his head. "The subject is closed."

Kermit stared at his father for a long moment, then sighed in defeat.

"What shall I tell Mother?"

"Edith will understand," said Roosevelt. "She has always understood. Tell her I'll send for her as soon as I've got a proper place to house us all." Suddenly he grinned again. "Maybe we should send for your sister Alice immediately. If there's any native opposition, she can terrify them into submission, just the way she used to do with my Cabinet."

"I'm being serious, Father."

"So am I, Kermit. America's never had an empire, and doesn't want one—but I made us a world power, and if I can increase our influence on a continent where we've yet to gain a foothold, then it's my duty to do so."

"And it'll be such fun," suggested Kermit knowingly.

Roosevelt flashed his son another grin. "It will be absolutely bully!"

Kermit stared at his father for a moment. "If I

can't talk you out of this enterprise, I wish you'd let me stay here with you."

Roosevelt shook his head. "Someone has to make sure all the trophies we've taken get to the American Museum on schedule. Besides, if we both stay here, the press will be sure I died during the safari. You've got to go back and tell them about the work I'm doing here." Suddenly he frowned. "Oh, and you'll have to see my editor at Scribner's and tell him that I'll be a little late on the safari manuscript. I'll start working on it as soon as we set up a permanent camp." He paused again. "Oh, yes. Before you woke up this morning, I gave a number of letters to Mr. Cunninghame, who will accompany you for the remainder of the journey. I want you to mail them when you get back to the States. The sooner we get some engineers and heavy equipment over here, the better."

"Heavy equipment?"

"Certainly. We've got a lot of land to clear and a railway to build." A superb starling walked boldly up to the mess tent, looking for scraps, and Roosevelt instantly withdrew his notebook and began scribbling again.

"The Congo's in the middle of the continent," Kermit pointed out. "It will be very difficult to bring in heavy equipment from the coast."

"Nonsense," scoffed Roosevelt. "The British disassembled their steamships, transported them in pieces, and then reassembled them on Lake Victoria and Lake Nyasa. Are you suggesting that Americans, who could build the Panama Canal and crisscross an entire continent with railroads, can't find a way to transport bulldozers and tractors to the Congo?" He paused. "You just see to it that those letters are delivered. The rest will take care of itself."

Just then Boyes approached them.

"Good morning, Mr. Boyes," said Roosevelt pleasantly. "Are we ready to leave?"

"We can break camp whenever you wish, Mr. President," said Boyes. "But one of our natives tells me there's a bull elephant carrying at least one hundred and thirty pounds a side not five miles from here."

"Really?" said Roosevelt, standing up excitedly. "Is he certain? I never saw ivory that large in Kenya."

"This particular boy's not wrong very often," answered Boyes. "He says this bull is surrounded by three or four *askaris*—young males—and that he's moving southeast. If we were to head off in *that* direction"—he pointed across the river to an expanse of dry, acacia-studded savannah—"we could probably catch up with him in a little less than three miles."

"Have we time?" asked Roosevelt, trying unsuccessfully to hide his eagerness.

Boyes smiled. "The Congo's been waiting for someone to civilize it for millions of years, Mr. President. I don't suppose another day will hurt."

Roosevelt turned to his son and shook his hand. "Have a safe trip, Kermit. If I bag this elephant, I'll have his tusks sent on after you."

"Good-bye, Father."

Roosevelt gave the young man a hug, and then went off to get his rifle.

"Don't worry, son," said Boyes, noting the young man's concern. "We'll take good care of your father. The next time you see him, he'll be the King of the Congo."

"President," Kermit corrected him.

"Whichever," said Boyes with a shrug.

III

IT TOOK ROOSEVELT SIX HOURS TO CATCH UP WITH HIS elephant, and the close stalk and kill took another hour. The rest of the day was spent removing the tusks and—at the ex-President's insistence—transporting almost three hundred pounds of elephant meat to the porters who had remained with Kermit.

It was too late to begin the trek to the Congo that day, but their little party was on the march shortly after sunrise the next morning. The savannah slowly changed to woodland, and finally, after six days, they came to the Mountains of the Moon.

"You're a remarkably fit man, Mr. President," remarked Boyes, as they made their first camp in a natural clearing by a small, clear stream at an altitude of about six thousand feet.

"A healthy mind and a healthy body go hand in

hand, John," replied Roosevelt. "It doesn't pay to ignore either of them."

"Still," continued Boyes, "once we cross the mountains, I think we'll try to find some blooded horses to ride."

"Blooded?" repeated Roosevelt.

"Horses that have already been bitten by the tsetse fly and survived," answered Boyes. "Once they've recovered from the disease, they're immune to it. Such animals are worth their weight in gold out here."

"Where will we find them, and how much will they cost?"

"Oh, the Belgian soldiers will have some," answered Boyes easily. "And they'll cost us two or three bullets."

"I don't understand."

Boyes grinned. "We'll kill a couple of elephants and trade the ivory for the horses."

"You're a resourceful man, Mr. Boyes," said Roosevelt with an appreciative grin.

"Out here a white man's either resourceful or he's dead," answered Boyes.

"I can well imagine," replied Roosevelt. He stared admiringly at the profusion of birds and monkeys that occupied the canopied forest that surrounded the clearing. "It's beautiful up here," he commented. "Pleasant days, brisk nights, fresh air, clear running water, game all around us. A man could spend his life right here."

"*Some* men could," said Boyes. "Not men like us."

"No," agreed Roosevelt with a sigh. "Not men like us."

"Still," continued Boyes, "there's no reason why we can't spend two or three days here. We'll be meeting our party on the other side of the mountains, but they probably won't arrive for another week to ten days. It will take time for word of our enterprise to circulate through the Lado."

"Good!" said Roosevelt. "It'll give me time to catch up on my writing." He paused. "By the way, where did you plan to pitch my tent?"

"Wherever you'd like it."

"As close to the stream as possible," answered Roosevelt. "It's really quite a lovely sight to wake up to."

"No reason why not," said Boyes. "I haven't seen any crocs or hippos about." He gave a brief command to the natives, and pointed to the spot Roosevelt had indicated.

"Please make sure the American flag is stationed in front of it," said Roosevelt. "Oh, and have my books placed inside it."

"You know," said Boyes, "we're using two boys just to carry your books, Mr. President. Perhaps we could leave some of them behind when we break camp and push inland."

Roosevelt shook his head. "That's out of the question: I'd be quite lost without access to literature. If we're short of manpower, we'll leave my rifle behind and have my gunbearer carry one of the book boxes."

"That won't be necessary, Mr. President. It was just a suggestion."

"Good," said Roosevelt with a smile. "Just between you and me, I'd feel almost as lost without my Winchester."

"You handle it very well."

"I'm just a talented amateur," answered Roosevelt. "I'm not in a class with you professional hunters."

Boyes laughed. "I'm no professional."

"You were hunting for ivory when we met."

"I was trying to increase my bank account," answered Boyes. "The ivory was just a means to an end. Karamojo Bell is a real hunter, or your friend Selous. I'm just an entrepreneur."

"Don't be so modest, John," said Roosevelt. "You managed to amass quite a pile of ivory. You couldn't do that if you weren't an expert hunter."

"Would you like to know how I actually went about collecting that ivory?" asked Boyes with a grin.

"Certainly."

"I don't know the first thing about tracking game, so I stopped at a British border post, explained that I was terrified of elephants, and slipped the border guards a few pounds to mark the major concentrations on a map of the Lado Enclave so I could avoid them."

Roosevelt laughed heartily. "Still, once you found the herds, you obviously knew what to do."

Boyes shrugged. "I just went where there was no competition."

"I thought the Enclave was filled with ivory hunters."

"Not in the shoulder-high grass," answered Boyes. "No way to sight your rifle, or to maneuver in case of a charge."

"How did you manage to hunt under such conditions?"

"I stood on my bearer's shoulders." Boyes chuckled at the memory. "The first few times I used a .475, but the recoil was so powerful that it knocked me off my perch each time I fired it, so in the end I wound up using a Lee-Enfield .303."

"You're a man of many talents, John."

A yellow-vented bulbul, bolder than its companions, suddenly landed in the clearing to more closely observe the pitching of the tents.

"Lovely bird, the bulbul," remarked Roosevelt, pulling out his notebook and entering the time and location where he had spotted it. "It has an absolutely beautiful voice, too."

"You're quite a bird-watcher, Mr. President," noted Boyes.

"Ornithology was my first love," answered Roosevelt. "I published my initial monograph on it when I was fourteen." He paused. "For the longest time, I thought my future would be in ornithology and taxidermy, but eventually I found men more interesting than animals." Suddenly he grinned. "Or at least, more in need of leadership."

"Well, we've come to the right place," replied Boyes. "I think the Congo is probably more in need of leadership than most places."

"That's what we're here for," agreed Roosevelt. "In fact, I think the time has come to begin formulating an approach to the problem. So far we've just been speaking in generalizations; we must have some definite plan to present to the men when we're fully assembled." He paused. "Let's take another look at that map."

Boyes withdrew a map from his pocket and unfolded it.

"This will never do," said Roosevelt, trying to

study the map as the wind kept whipping through it. "Let's find a table."

Boyes ordered two of the natives to set up a table and a pair of chairs, and a moment later he and Roosevelt were sitting side by side, with the map laid out on the table and held in place by four small rocks.

"Where are we now?" asked Roosevelt.

"Right about here, sir," answered Boyes, pointing to their location. "The mountains are the dividing line between Uganda and the Congo. We'll have to concentrate our initial efforts in the eastern section."

"Why?" asked Roosevelt. "If we move *here*"—he pointed to a more centrally-located spot—"we'll have access to the Congo River."

"Not practical," answered Boyes. "Most of the tribes in the eastern quarter of the country understand Swahili, and that's the only native language most of our men will be able to speak. Once we get inland we'll run into more than two hundred dialects, and if they speak any civilized language at all, it'll be French, not English."

"I see," said Roosevelt. He paused to consider this information, then stared at the map again. "Now, where does the East African Railway terminate?"

"Over here," said Boyes, pointing. "In Kampala, about halfway through Uganda."

"So we'll have to extend the railway or build a road about three hundred miles or more to reach a base in the eastern section of the Congo?"

"That's a very ambitious undertaking, Mr. President," said Boyes dubiously.

"Still, it will have to be done. There's no other way

to bring in the equipment we'll need." Roosevelt turned to Boyes. "You look doubtful, John."

"It could take years. The East African Railway wasn't called the Lunatic Line without cause."

Roosevelt smiled confidently. "They called it the Lunatic Line because only a lunatic would spend one thousand pounds per mile of track. Well, if there's one thing Americans can build, it's railroads. We'll do it for a tenth of the cost in a fiftieth of the time."

"If you extend it from Kampala, you'll have to run it over the Mountains of the Moon," noted Boyes.

"We ran railroads over the Rocky Mountains almost half a century ago," said Roosevelt, dismissing the subject. "Now, are there any major cities in the eastern sector? Where's Stanleyville?"

"Stanleyville could be on a different planet, for all the commerce it has with the eastern Congo," replied Boyes. "In fact, most of the Belgian settlements are along the Congo River"—he pointed out the river—"which, as you can see, doesn't extend to the eastern section. There are no railways, no rivers, and no roads connecting the eastern sector to the settlements." He paused. "Initially, this may very well work to our advantage, as it could be months before news of anything we may do will reach them."

"Then what *is* in the east?"

Boyes shrugged. "Animals and savages."

"We'll leave the animals alone and elevate the savages," said Roosevelt. "What's the major tribe there?"

"The Mangbetu."

"Do you know anything about them?"

"Just that they're as warlike as the Maasai and the

Zulu. They've conquered most of the other tribes."
He paused. "And they're supposed to be cannibals."

"We'll have to put a stop to that," said Roosevelt.
He flashed Boyes another grin. "We can't have them
going around eating registered voters."

"Especially Republicans?" suggested Boyes with
a chuckle.

"Especially Republicans," agreed Roosevelt. He
paused. "Have they had much commerce with white
men?"

"The Belgians leave them pretty much alone," answered Boyes. "They killed the first few civil servants who paid them a visit."

"Then it would be reasonable to assume that they
will be unresponsive to our peaceful overtures?"

"I think you could say so, yes."

"Then perhaps we can draw upon your expertise,
John," said Roosevelt. "After all, Kikuyuland was
also hostile to white men when you first entered it."

"It was a different situation," explained Boyes.
"They were warring among themselves, so I simply
placed myself and my gun at the disposal of one of
the weaker clans and made myself indispensable to
them. Once word got out that I had sided with them
and turned the tide of battle, they knew they'd be
massacred if I left, so they begged me to stay, and
one by one we began assimilating the other Kikuyu
clans until we had unified the entire nation." He
paused. "The Mangbetu are already united, and I
very much doubt that they would appreciate any
interference from us." He stared thoughtfully at
Roosevelt. "And there's something else."

"What?"

"I didn't enter Kikuyuland to bring them the benefits of civilization. The East African Railway needed supplies for twenty-five thousand coolie laborers, and all I wanted to do was find a cheap source of food that I could resell. I was just trying to make a living, not to change the way the Kikuyu lived." He paused. "African natives are a very peculiar lot. You can shoot their elephants, pull gold and diamonds out of their land, even buy their slaves, and they don't seem to give a damn. But once you start interfering with the way they live, you've got a real problem on your hands."

"There's an enormous difference between American democracy and European colonialism," said Roosevelt firmly.

"Let's hope the residents of the Congo agree, sir," said Boyes wryly.

"They will," said Roosevelt. "You know, John, this enterprise was initially your suggestion. If you feel this way, why have you volunteered to help me?"

"I've made and lost three fortunes on this continent," answered Boyes bluntly. "Some gut instinct tells me that there's another one to be made in the Congo. Besides," he added with a smile, "it sounds like a bully adventure."

Roosevelt laughed at Boyes' use of his favorite term. "Well, at least you're being honest, and I can't ask for more than that. Now let's get back to work." He paused, ordering his thoughts. "It seems to me that as long as the Mangbetu control the area, it makes sense to work through them, to use them as our surrogates until we can educate *all* the natives."

"I suppose so," said Boyes. "Still, we can't just walk in there, tell them that we're bringing them the advantages of civilization, and expect a friendly reception."

"Why not?" said Roosevelt confidently. "The direct approach is usually best."

"They're predisposed to dislike and distrust you, Mr. President."

"They're predisposed to dislike and distrust Belgians, John," answered Roosevelt. "They've never met an American before."

"I don't think they're inclined to differentiate between white men," said Boyes.

"You're viewing them as Democrats," said Roosevelt with a smile. "I prefer to think of them as uncommitted voters."

"I think you'd be better advised to think of them as hostile—and hungry."

"John, when I was President, I used to have a saying: Walk softly, but carry a big stick."

"I've heard it," acknowledged Boyes.

"Well, I intend to walk softly among the Mangbetu—but if worst comes to worst, we'll be carrying fifty big sticks with us."

"I wonder if fifty guns will be enough," said Boyes, frowning.

"We're not coming to slaughter them, John—merely to impress them."

"We might impress them more if we waited for some of your engineers and Rough Riders to show up."

"Time is a precious commodity," answered Roosevelt. "I have never believed in wasting it." He paused. "Bill Taft will almost certainly run for reelection in 1912. I'd like to make him a gift of the

Congo as an American protectorate before he leaves office."

"You expect to civilize this whole country in six years?" asked Boyes in amused disbelief.

"Why not?" answered Roosevelt seriously. "God made the whole world in just six days, didn't He?"

IV

THEY REMAINED IN CAMP FOR TWO DAYS, WITH ROOSEVELT becoming more and more restless to begin his vast undertaking. Finally he convinced Boyes to trek across the mountain range, and a week later they set up a base camp on the eastern border of the Belgian Congo.

The ex-President was overflowing with energy. When Boyes would awaken at sunrise, Roosevelt had already written ten or twelve pages, and was undergoing his daily regimen of vigorous exercise. By nine in the morning he was too restless to remain in camp, and he would take a tracker and a bearer out to hunt some game for the pot. In the heat of the day, while Boyes and the porters slept in the shade, Roosevelt sat in a canvas chair beside his tent, reading from the sixty-volume library that accompanied him everywhere. By late afternoon it was time for a long walk and an hour of serious bird-watching, followed by still more writing and then dinner. And always, as he sat beside the fire with Boyes and those poachers who had begun making their way to the base camp, he would speak for hours, firing them with his vision for the Congo and discussing how best to accomplish it. Then, somewhere between nine and ten at night, everyone would go off to bed, and while the others slept, Roosevelt's tent was aglow with lantern light as he read for another hour.

Boyes decided that if Roosevelt weren't given something substantial to do he might spontaneously combust with nervous energy. Therefore, since thirty-three members of his little company had already arrived, he broke camp and assumed that the remaining fifteen to twenty men would be able to follow their trail.

They spent two days tracking down a large bull elephant and his young *askaris*; came away with fourteen tusks, six of them quite large; and then marched them twenty miles north to a Belgian outpost. They traded the tusks for seven blooded horses, left three of their party behind to acquire more ivory and trade it for the necessary number of horses, and then headed south into Mangbetu country.

They were quite a group. There was Deaf Banks, who had lost his hearing from proximity to repeated elephant gun explosions, but had refused to quit Africa or even leave the bush, and had shot more than five hundred elephants. There was Bill Buckley, a burly Englishman who had given up his gold mine in Rhodesia for the white gold he found farther north. There was Mickey Norton, who had spent a grand total of three days in cities during the past twenty years. There was Charlie Ross, who had left his native Australia to become a Canadian Mountie, then decided that the life was too tame and emigrated to Africa. There was Billy Pickering, who had already served two sentences in Belgian jails for ivory poaching, and had his own notions concerning how to civilize the Congo. There were William and Richard Brittlebanks, brothers who had found hunting in the Klondike to be too cold for their taste, and had been poaching ivory in the Sudan for the better part of a decade. There was even an American, Yank Rogers, one of Roosevelt's former Rough Riders, who had no use for the British or the Belgians, but joined up the moment he heard that his beloved Teddy was looking for volunteers. Only the fabled Karamojo Bell, who had just killed his 962nd elephant and was eager to finally bag his thousandth, refused to leave the Lado.

It was understood from the start that Boyes was Roosevelt's lieutenant, and the few who chose to argue the point soon found out just how much strength and determination lay hidden within his scrawny, five-foot two-inch body. After a pair of fistfights and a threatened pistol duel, which Roosevelt himself had to break up, the chain of command was never again challenged.

They began marching south and west, moving farther from the border and into more heavily-forested territory as they sought out the Mangbetu. By the time a week had passed, eighteen more men had joined them.

On the eighth day they came to a large village. The huts were made of dried cattle dung, with thatched roofs, and were clustered around a large central compound.

The inhabitants still spoke Swahili, and explained that the Mangbetu territory was another two days' march to the south. Boyes had the Brittlebanks brothers shoot a couple of bushbuck and a duiker, and made a gift of the meat to the village. He promised to bring them still more meat upon their return, explaining to Roosevelt that this was a standard practice, as one never knew when one might need a friendly village while beating a hasty retreat.

Roosevelt was eager to meet the Mangbetu, and he got his wish two mornings later, shortly after sunrise, when they came upon a Mangbetu village in a large clearing by a river.

"I wonder how many white men they've seen before?" said Roosevelt as a couple of hundred painted Mangbetu, some of them wearing blankets and leopardskin cloaks in the cold morning air, gathered in the center of the village, brandishing their spears and staring at the approaching party.

"They've probably eaten their fair share of Belgians," replied Boyes. "At any rate, they'll know what a rifle is, so we'd better display them."

"They can see that we have them," answered Roosevelt. "That's enough."

"But sir—"

"We've come to befriend them, not decimate them, John. Keep the men back here so they don't feel that we're threatening them," ordered Roosevelt.

"Mr. President, sir," protested Mickey Norton, "please listen to me. I've had experience dealing with savages. We all have. You've got to show 'em who's boss."

"They're not savages, Mr. Norton," said Roosevelt.

"Then what *are* they?"

Roosevelt grinned. "Voters." He climbed down off his horse. "They're our constituents, and I think I'd like to meet them on equal footing."

"Then you'd better take off all your clothes and get a spear."

"That will be enough, Mr. Norton," said Roosevelt firmly.

One old man, wearing a headdress made of a lion's mane and ostrich feathers, seated himself on a stool outside the largest hut, and a number of warriors immediately positioned themselves in front of him.

"Would that be the chief?" asked Roosevelt.

"Probably," said Boyes. "Once in a while, you get a real smart chief who puts someone else on the throne and disguises himself as a warrior, just in case you're here to kill him. But since the Mangbetu rule this territory, I think we can assume that he's really the headman."

"Nice headdress," commented Roosevelt admiringly. He handed his rifle to Norton. "John, leave your gun behind and come with me. The rest of you men, wait here."

"Would you like us to fan out around the village, sir?" suggested Charlie Ross.

Roosevelt shook his head. "If they've seen rifles before, it won't be necessary, and if they haven't, then it wouldn't do any good."

"Is there anything we *can* do, sir?"

"Try smiling," answered Roosevelt. "Come on, John."

They began approaching the cluster of warriors. A dog raced up, barking furiously. Roosevelt ignored it, and when it saw that it had failed to intimidate them, it lay down in the dust with an almost human expression of disappointment on its face and watched the two men walk past.

The warriors began murmuring, softly at first, then louder, and someone began beating a primal rhythm on the drum.

"The Lado is looking better and better with every step we take," commented Boyes under his breath.

"They're just people, John," Roosevelt assured him.

"With very unusual dietary habits," muttered Boyes.

"If you're worried, I can always have Yank act as my interpreter."

"I'm not worried about dying," answered Boyes. "I just don't want to go down in the history books as the man who led Teddy Roosevelt into a Mangbetu cooking pot."

Roosevelt chuckled. "If it happens, there won't be any survivors to write about it. Now try to be a little more optimistic." He looked ahead at the assembled Mangbetu. "What do you suppose would happen if we walked right up to the chief?"

"He's got a couple of pretty mean-looking young bucks standing on each side of him," noted Boyes. "I wish we had our rifles."

"We won't need them, John," Roosevelt assured him. "I was always surrounded by the Secret Service when I was President—but they never interfered with my conduct of my office."

They were close enough now to smell the various oils that the Mangbetu had rubbed onto their bodies, and to see some of the patterns that had been tattooed onto their faces and torsos.

"Just keep smiling," answered Roosevelt. "We're unarmed, and our men are keeping their distance."

"Why do we have to smile?" asked Boyes.

"First, to show that we're happy to see them," said Roosevelt. "And second, to show them that we don't file our teeth."

The Mangbetu brandished their spears threateningly as Roosevelt reached them, but the old headman uttered a single command and they parted, allowing the two men a narrow path to the chief. When they got to within eight feet of him, however, four large bodyguards stepped forward and barred their way.

"John, tell him that I'm the King of America, and that I bring him greetings and felicitations."

Boyes translated Roosevelt's message. The chief stared impassively at him, and the four warriors did not relax their posture.

"Tell him that my country has no love for the Belgians."

Boyes uttered something in Swahili, and suddenly the old man seemed to show some interest. He nodded his head and responded.

"He says he's got no use for them either."

Roosevelt's smile broadened. "Tell him we're going to be great friends."

Boyes spoke to the chief again. "He wants to know why."

"Because I am going to bring him all the gifts of civilization, and I ask nothing in return except his friendship."

Another brief exchange followed. "He wants to know where the gifts of civilization are."

"Tell him they're too big for our small party of men to carry, but they're on their way."

The chief listened, finally flashed Roosevelt a smile, and turned to Boyes.

"He says any enemy of the Belgians is a friend of his."

Roosevelt stepped forward and extended his hand. The chief stared at it for a moment, then hesitantly held out his own. Roosevelt took it and shook it vigorously. Two of the old man's bodyguards tensed and raised their spears again, but the chief said something to them and they immediately backed off.

"I think you startled them," offered Boyes.

"A good politician always likes to press the flesh, as we say back home," responded Roosevelt. "Tell him that we're going to bring democracy to the Congo."

"There's no word for *democracy* in Swahili."

"What's the closest approximation?"

"There isn't one."

The chief suddenly began speaking. Boyes listened for a moment, then turned to Roosevelt.

"He suggests that our men leave their weapons behind and come join him in a feast celebrating our friendship."

"What do you think?"

"Maybe he's as friendly as he seems, but I don't think it would be a good idea just yet."

"All right," responded Roosevelt, holding his hand up to his glasses as a breeze brought a cloud of dust with it. "Thank him, tell him that the men have already eaten, but that you and I will accept his gracious invitation while our men guard the village against the approach of any Belgians."

"He says there aren't any Belgians in the area."

"Tell him we didn't see any either, but one can't be too careful in these dangerous times, and that now that we are friends, our men are prepared to die defending his village from his Belgian oppressors."

The chief seemed somewhat mollified, and nodded his acquiescence.

"Did you ever drink *pombe*?" asked Boyes, as the chief arose and invited them into his hut.

"No," said Roosevelt. "What is it?"

"A native beer."

"You know I don't imbibe stimulants, John."

"Well, Mr. President, you're going to have to learn how to imbibe very fast, or you're going to offend our host."

"Nonsense, John," said Roosevelt. "This is a democracy. Every man is free to drink what he wants."

"Since when did it become a democracy?" asked Boyes wryly.

"Since you and I were invited to partake in dinner, rather than constitute it," said Roosevelt. "Now let's go explain all the wonders we're going to bring to the Congo."

"Has it occurred to you that you ought to be speaking to the *people* about democracy, rather than to the hereditary chief?" suggested Boyes wryly.

"You've never seen me charm the opposition, John," said Roosevelt with a confident smile. He walked to the door of the hut, then lowered his head and entered the darkened interior. "Give me three hours with him and he'll be our biggest supporter."

He was wrong. It only took ninety minutes.

V

THEY SPENT THE NEXT TWO WEEKS MARCHING DEEPER INTO
Mangbetu territory. News of their arrival always
preceded them, transmitted by huge, eight-foot
drums, and their reception was always cordial, so
much so that after the first four encounters Roosevelt allowed all of his men to enter the villages.

By their eighth day in Mangbetu country the remainder of their party had caught up with them,
bringing enough horses so that all fifty-three men
were mounted. Boyes assigned rotating shifts to construct camps, cook, and hunt for meat, and Roosevelt spent every spare minute trying to master
Swahili. He forbade anyone to speak to him in English, and within two weeks he was able to make
himself understood to the Mangbetu, although it was
another month before he could discuss his visions of
a democratic Congo without the aid of a translator.

"A wonderful people!" he exclaimed one night as he, Boyes, Charlie Ross, and Billy Pickering sat by one of the campfires, after having enlisted yet another two thousand Mangbetu to their cause. "Clean, bright, willing to listen to new ideas. I have high hopes for our crusade, John."

Boyes threw a stone at a pair of hyenas that had been attracted by the smell of the impala they had eaten for dinner, and they raced off into the darkness, yelping and giggling.

"I don't know," he replied. "Everything's gone smoothly so far, but . . ."

"But what?"

"These people don't have the slightest idea what you're talking about, Mr. President," said Boyes bluntly.

"I was going to mention that myself," put in Charlie Ross.

"Certainly they do," said Roosevelt. "I spent the entire afternoon with Matapoli—that was his name, wasn't it?—and his elders, explaining how we were going to bring democracy to the Congo. Didn't you see how enthused they all were?"

"There's still no word for *democracy* in Swahili," answered Boyes. "They probably think it's something to eat."

"You underestimate them, John."

"I've lived among blacks all my adult life," replied Boyes. "If anything, I tend to over-estimate them."

Roosevelt shook his head. "The problem is cultural, not racial. In America, we have many Negroes who have become doctors, lawyers, scientists, even politicians. There is nothing a white man can do that a Negro can't do, given the proper training and opportunity."

"Maybe American blacks," said Billy Pickering. "But not Africans."

Roosevelt chuckled in amusement. "Just where do you think America's Negroes came from, Mr. Pickering?"

"Not from the Congo, that's for sure," said Pickering adamantly. "Maybe West African blacks are different."

"All men are pretty much the same, if they are given the same opportunities," said Roosevelt.

"I disagree," said Boyes. "I became the King of the Kikuyu, and you're probably going to become President of the Congo. You don't see any blacks becoming king or president of white countries, do you?"

"Give them time, John, and they will."

"I'll believe it when I see it."

"You may not live to see it, and I may not," said Roosevelt. "But one of these days it's going to happen. Take my word for it."

A lion coughed about a hundred yards away. Both men ignored it.

"Well, you're a very learned man, so if you say it's going to happen, then I suppose it is," said Boyes. "But I hope you're also right that I'll be dead and buried when that happy day occurs."

"You know," mused Roosevelt, "maybe I ought to urge some of our American Negroes to come over here. They could become the first generation of congressmen, so to speak."

"A bunch of your freed slaves set up shop in Liberia a few years back," noted Charlie Ross. "The first thing they did was to start rounding up all the native Liberians and sell them into slavery." He snorted contemptuously. "Some democracy."

"This will be different, Mr. Ross," responded Roosevelt. "These will be educated American politicians, who also just happen to be Negroes."

"Their heads would be decorating every village from here to the Sudan a week later," said Pickering with absolute certainty.

"The Belgians may be oppressing the natives now," added Boyes, "but as soon as they leave, it'll be back to tribal warfare as usual." He paused. "Your democracy is going to have exactly as many political parties as there are tribes, no more and no less, and no tribal member will ever vote for anyone other than a tribal brother."

"Nonsense!" scoffed Roosevelt. "If that philosophy held true, I'd never have won a single vote outside of my home state of New York."

"We're not in America, Mr. President," responded Boyes.

"I obviously have more faith in these people than you do, John."

"Maybe that's because I know them better."

Suddenly Roosevelt grinned. "Well, it wouldn't be any fun if it was *too* easy, would it?"

Boyes smiled wryly. "I think you're in for a little more fun than you bargained for."

"God put us here to meet challenges."

"Oh," said Charlie Ross. "I was *wondering* why He put us here."

"That's blasphemy, Mr. Ross," said Roosevelt sternly. "I won't hear any more of it."

The men fell silent, and a few moments later, when

the fire started dying down, Roosevelt went off to his tent to read.

"He's biting off more than he can chew, John," said Billy Pickering when the ex-President was out of earshot.

"Maybe," said Boyes noncommittally.

"There's no maybe about it," said Pickering. "He hasn't lived with Africans. *We* have. You know what they're like."

"There's another problem, too, John," added Ross.

"Oh?" said Boyes.

"I have a feeling he thinks of us as the Rough Riders, all in for the long haul. But the long rains are coming in a couple of months, and I've got to get my ivory to Mombasa before then. So do a lot of the others."

"You're making a big mistake, Charlie," said Boyes. "He's offering us a whole country. There's not just ivory here; there's gold and silver and copper as well, and *somebody* is going to have to administer it. If you leave now, we may not let you come back."

"You'd stop me?" asked Ross, amused.

"I've got no use for deserters," answered Boyes seriously.

"I never signed any enlistment papers. How can I be a deserter?"

"You can be a deserter by leaving the President when he needs every man he can get."

"Look, John," said Ross. "If I thought there was one chance in a hundred that he could pull this off, I'd stay, no question about it. But we've all managed to accumulate some ivory, and we've had a fine time together, and we haven't had to fight the Belgians yet. Maybe it's time to think about pulling out, while we're still ahead of the game."

Boyes shook his head. "He's a great man, Charlie, and he's capable of great things."

"Even if he does what he says he's going to do, do you really want to live in the Congo forever?"

"I'll live anywhere the pickings are easy," answered Boyes. "And if you're smart, so will you."

"I'll have to think about it, John," said Ross, getting up and heading off toward his tent.

"How about you, Billy?" asked Boyes.

"I came here for just one reason," answered Pickering. "To kill Belgians. We haven't seen any yet, so I guess I'll stick around a little longer." Then he, too, got up and walked away.

The little Yorkshireman remained by the dying embers for a few more minutes, wondering just how much time Roosevelt had before everything fell apart.

VI

Two months into what Roosevelt termed their "bully undertaking" they finally ran into some organized resistance. To nobody's great surprise, it came not from the various tribes they had been enlisting in their project, but from the Belgian colonial government.

Despite the imminent arrival of the long rains, Roosevelt's entire party was still in the Congo, due mostly to the threats, pleadings, and promises of riches that Boyes had made when the ex-President was out of earshot.

They had made their way through a dense forest and were now camped by a winding, crocodile-infested river. A dozen of the men were out hunting for ivory, and Pickering was scouting about thirty miles to the west with a Mangbetu guide, seeking a location for their next campsite. Three more members of the party were visiting large Mangbetu villages, scheduling visits from the "King of America" and arranging for word to be passed to the leaders of the smaller villages, most of whom wanted to come and listen to him speak of the wonders he planned to bring to the Congo.

Roosevelt was sitting on a canvas chair in front of his tent, his binoculars hung around his neck and a sheaf of papers laid out on a table before him, editing what he had written that morning, when Yank Rogers, clad in his trademark stovepipe chaps and cowboy Stetson, approached him.

"We got company, Teddy," he announced in his gentle Texas drawl.

"Oh?"

Rogers nodded. "Belgians—and they look like they're ready to declare war before lunch."

"Mr. Pickering will be heartbroken when he finds out," remarked Roosevelt wryly. He wiped some sweat from his face with a handkerchief. "Send them away, and tell them we'll only speak to the man in charge."

"In charge of what?" asked Rogers, puzzled.

"The Congo," answered Roosevelt. "We're going to have to meet him sooner or later. Why should we march all the way to Stanleyville?"

"What if they insist?"

"How big is their party?" asked Roosevelt.

"One guy in a suit, six in uniforms," said Rogers.

"Take twenty of our men with you, and make sure they're all carrying their rifles. The Belgians won't insist."

"Right, Teddy."

"Oh, and Yank?"

The American stopped. "Yes?"

"Tell Mr. Boyes not to remove their wallets before they leave."

Rogers grinned. "That little bastard could find an angle on a baseball. You know he's taking ten percent off the top on all the ivory our men shoot?"

"No, I didn't know. Has anyone objected?"

"Not since he went up against Big Bill Buckley and gave him a whipping," laughed Wallace. "I think he's got notions of taking a percentage of every tusk that's shipped out of the Congo from now till Doomsday." He paused. "Well, I'd better round up a posse and go have a pow-wow with our visitors."

"Do that," said Roosevelt, spotting an insect that was crawling across his papers and flicking it to the ground. "And send Mr. Boyes over here. I think I'd better have a talk with him."

"If you're going to fight him, I think I can get three-to-one on you," said Rogers. "The rest of 'em never saw you take out that machine gun nest single-handed at San Juan Hill; *I* did. Want me to put a little something down for you, Teddy?"

Roosevelt chuckled at the thought. "Maybe a pound or two, if it comes to that. Which," he added seriously, "it won't."

Rogers went off to gather some of the men, and a few minutes later Boyes approached Roosevelt's tent.

"You wanted to see me, Mr. President?" he asked.

"Yes, I did, John."

"Is it anything to do with the Belgians? Yank Rogers said you were sending them away."

"They'll be back," said Roosevelt, wiping his face once again and wondering if he'd ever experienced this much humidity anywhere in America. "Pull up a chair, John."

Boyes did so, and sat down opposite Roosevelt.

"John, Yank tells me that you've got a healthy little business going on here."

"You mean the ivory?" asked Boyes, making no attempt to conceal it.

Roosevelt nodded. "We're not here to get rich, John. We're here to turn the Congo into a democracy."

"There's no law against doing both," said Boyes.

"I strongly disapprove of it, John. It's profiteering."

"I'm not making a single shilling off the natives, Mr. President," protested Boyes. "How can that be profiteering?"

"You're making it off our own people," said Roosevelt. "That's just as bad."

"I was afraid you were going to look at it like that," said Boyes with a sigh. "Look, Mr. President, we're all for civilizing the Congo—but we're grown men, and we've got to make a living. Now, for most of them, that means ivory hunting when we're not busy befriending the natives. Believe me when I tell you that if you were to forbid it, eighty percent of the men would leave."

"I believe you, John," said Roosevelt. "And I haven't stopped them from hunting ivory whenever they've had the time."

"Well, I haven't got any spare time, between running the camp and acting as your second-in-command," continued Boyes, "so if I'm to make any money, it can't be by spending long days in the bush, hunting for ivory. So unless you see fit to pay me a salary, this seems the most reasonable way of earning some money. It doesn't cost you anything, it doesn't cost the natives anything, and every one of our men knew the conditions before they signed on."

Roosevelt considered Boyes' argument for a moment, then nodded his consent.

"All right, John. Far be it from me to stand in the way of an entrepreneur." He paused for a moment. "But I want you to promise me one thing."

"What?"

"You'll let me know before you indulge in any other plans to get rich."

"Oh, I'm never without plans, Mr. President," Boyes assured him.

"Would you care to confide in me, then?"

"Why not?" replied Boyes with a shrug. "I've got nothing to hide." He leaned forward in his chair. "Once you start putting your railroad through here, you're going to need about ten thousand laborers. Now, I don't know if you're going to draft some workers from the local tribes, or hire a bunch of coolies from British East, or import all your labor from America—but I *do* know that ten thousand men eat a lot of food. I thought I'd set up a little trading company to deal with some of the tribes; you know, give them things they want in exchange for bags of flour and other edibles." He paused. "It'll be the same thing I did with the Kikuyu when they built the Lunatic Line, and I kept twenty-five thousand coolies fed for the better part of two years."

"I don't want you fleecing the same people we're trying to befriend," said Roosevelt. "We're here to liberate this country, not plunder it."

"If they don't like what I have to trade, they don't

have to part with their goods," said Boyes. "And if they *do* like it, I'll undersell any competitor by fifty percent, which will save your fledgling treasury a lot of money."

Roosevelt stared at him for a long moment.

"Well?" said Boyes at last.

"John, if you can save us that much money without cheating the natives, get as rich as you like."

Boyes smiled. "I don't mind if I do, Mr. President."

"You're a remarkable man, John."

Boyes shook his head. "I'm just a skinny little guy who had to learn to use his head to survive with all these brawny white hunters."

"I understand you gave one of them quite a lesson in fisticuffs," remarked Roosevelt.

"You mean Buckley? I had no choice in the matter," answered Boyes. "If I'd let him get away with it, by next week they'd all be backing out on their bargain." Suddenly he smiled again. "I gave him a bottle of gin and helped him finish it, and by the next morning we were good friends again."

"You're in the wrong profession, John," said Roosevelt. "You should have been a politician."

"Not enough money in it," answered Boyes bluntly. "But while we're on the subject of politics, why did we run the Belgians off? Sooner or later we're going to have to deal with them."

"It's simply a matter of practicality," answered Roosevelt. "I think we gave them enough of an insult that the governor of the Congo will have to come here in person to prove that we can't get away with such behavior—and the sooner we meet with him, the sooner we can present our demands."

"What, exactly, do we plan to demand?"

"We're going to demand their complete withdrawal from the Congo, and we're going to stipulate that they must make a public statement in the world press that they no longer have any colonial ambitions in Africa."

"You're not asking for much, are you?" said Boyes sardonically.

"The Belgians have no use for it, and it costs them a fortune to administer it." Roosevelt paused. "King Albert can go find another hunting reserve. We've got a nation to build here."

Boyes laughed in amusement. "And you think they're going to turn it over to a force of fifty-three men?"

"Certainly not," said Roosevelt. "They're going to turn it over to the natives who live here."

Boyes stared intently at Roosevelt. "You're serious, aren't you?"

"That *is* what we've come here for, isn't it?"

"Yes, but—"

"We have a job to do, John, and time is the one irreplaceable commodity in this world. We can't afford to waste it."

"Are you sure you're not being a little premature about this, Mr. President?" asked Boyes. "I thought we'd spend a year building a native army, and—"

"We can't win a war with the Belgians, John."

"Then what kind of pressure can you bring to bear on them?" asked Boyes, puzzled.

"We can threaten to *lose* a war with them."

Boyes frowned. "I don't think I quite understand, sir."

"You will, John," said Roosevelt confidently. "You will."

118

VII

IT TOOK THE ASSISTANT GOVERNOR OF THE CONGO exactly seven weeks to hear of Roosevelt's summary
dismissal of his district representative and to trek
from Stanleyville to the American's base camp, by
which time the rains had come and gone and the ex-
President had enlisted not only the entire Mangbetu
nation to his cause, but seven lesser tribes as well.

Word of the Belgians' impending arrival reached
camp a full week before they actually showed up—
"God, I love those drums!" was Roosevelt's only
comment—and Yank Rogers and the Brittlebanks
brothers were sent out to greet the party and escort
them back to camp.

Roosevelt ordered Boyes to send five of their men
out on a two-week hunting expedition. When the little Yorkshireman asked what they were supposed to
be hunting for, Roosevelt replied that he didn't much

care, as long as they were totally out of communication for at least fourteen days. Boyes shrugged, scratched his head, and finally selected five of his companions at random and suggested they do a little ivory hunting far to the south for the two weeks. Since they had virtually shot out the immediate area, he received no objections.

When the Belgian party finally reached the camp, Roosevelt was waiting for them. He had had his men construct a huge table, some thirty feet long and five feet wide, and the moment they dismounted he invited them to join him and his men for lunch. The assistant governor, a tall, lean, ambitious man named Gerard Silva, seemed somewhat taken aback by the American's hospitality, but allowed himself and his twenty armed soldiers to be escorted to the table, where a truly magnificent feast of warthog, bushbuck, and guinea fowl awaited them.

Roosevelt's men, such as could fit on one side of the table, sat facing the west, and the Belgian soldiers were seated opposite them. The American sat at the head of the table, and Silva sat at the foot of it, thirty feet away. Under such an arrangement, private discussion between the two leaders was impossible, and Roosevelt encouraged his men to discuss their hunting and exploring adventures, though not more than half a dozen of the Belgian soldiers could speak or understand English.

Finally, after almost two hours, the meal was concluded, and Roosevelt's men—except for Boyes—left the table one by one. Silva nodded to a young lieutenant, and the Belgian solders followed suit, clustering awkwardly around their horses. Then Silva stood up, walked down to Roosevelt's end of the table, and seated himself next to the American.

"I hope you enjoyed your meal, Mr. Silva," said Roosevelt, sipping a cup of tea.

"It was quite excellent, Mr...?" Silva paused. "What would you prefer that I call you?"

"Colonel Roosevelt, Mr. Roosevelt, or Mr. President, as you prefer," said Roosevelt expansively.

"It was an excellent meal, Mr. Roosevelt," said Silva in precise, heavily-accented English. He withdrew a cigar and offered one to Roosevelt, who refused it. "A wise decision," he said. "The tobacco we grow here is decidedly inferior."

"You must be anxious to return to Belgium, then," suggested Roosevelt.

"As you must be anxious to return to America," responded Silva.

"Actually, I like it here," said Roosevelt. "But then, I don't smoke."

"A nasty habit," admitted Silva. "But then, so is trespassing."

"*Am* I trespassing?" asked Roosevelt innocently.

"Do not be coy with me, Mr. Roosevelt," said Silva. "It is most unbecoming. You have brought a force of men into Belgian territory for reasons that have not been made clear to us. You have no hunting permit, no visa, no permission to be here at all."

"Are you telling us to leave?"

"I am simply trying to discover your purpose here," said Silva. "If you have come solely for sport, I will personally present you with papers that will allow you to go anywhere you wish within the Congo. If you have come for some other reason, I demand to know what it is."

"I would rather discuss that with the governor himself," responded Roosevelt.

"He is quite ill with malaria, and may not be able to leave Stanleyville for another month."

Roosevelt considered the statement for a moment, then shook his head. "No, we've wasted enough time already. I suppose you'll simply have to take my message to him." He paused. "I suppose it doesn't make much difference. The only thing he'll do is transmit my message to King Albert."

"And what is the gist of your message, Mr. Roosevelt?" asked Silva, leaning forward intently.

"My men and I don't consider ourselves to be in Belgian territory."

Silva smiled humorlessly. "Perhaps you would like me to pinpoint your position on a map. You are indeed within the legal boundaries of the Belgian Congo."

"We know where we are, and we fully agree that we are inside the border of the Congo," answered Roosevelt. "But we don't recognize your authority here."

"Here? You mean right where we are sitting?"

"I mean anywhere in the Congo."

"The Congo is Belgian territory, Mr. Roosevelt."

Roosevelt shook his head. "The Congo belongs to its inhabitants. It's time they began determining their own future."

"That is the most ridiculous thing I have ever heard," said Silva. "It has been acknowledged by all the great powers that the Congo is our colony."

"All but one," said Roosevelt.

"America acknowledges our right to the Congo."

"America has a history of opposing imperialism

wherever we find it," replied Roosevelt. "We threw the British out of our own country, and we're fully prepared to throw the Belgians out of the Congo."

"Just as, when you were President, you threw the Panamanians out of Panama?" asked Silva sardonically.

"America has no imperial claim to Panama. The Panamanians have their own government and we recognize it." Roosevelt paused. "However, we're not talking about Panama, but about the Congo."

Silva stared at Roosevelt. "For whom do you speak, Mr. Roosevelt?" asked Silva. "You are no longer President, so surely you do not speak for America."

"I speak for the citizens of the Congo."

Silva laughed contemptuously. "They are a bunch of savages who have no interest whatsoever in who rules them."

"Would you care to put that to a vote?" asked Roosevelt with a smile.

"So they vote now?"

"Not yet," answered Roosevelt. "But they will as soon as they are free to do so."

"And who will set them free?"

"*We* will," interjected Boyes from his seat halfway down the table.

"*You* will?" repeated Silva, turning to face Boyes. "I've heard about you, John Boyes. You have been in trouble with every government from South Africa to Abyssinia."

"I don't get along well with colonial governments," replied Boyes.

"You don't get along well with native governments, either," said Silva. He turned to Roosevelt.

"Did you know that your companion talked the ignorant natives who proclaimed him their king into selling him Mount Kenya for the enormous price of four goats?"

"Six," Boyes corrected him with a smile. "I wouldn't want it said that I was cheap."

"This is ridiculous!" said Silva in exasperation. "I cannot believe I am hearing this! Do you really propose to conquer the Belgian Congo with a force of fifty-three men?"

"Absolutely not," said Roosevelt pleasantly.

"Well, then?"

"First," said Roosevelt, "it is the Congo, not the Belgian Congo. Second, we don't propose to conquer it, but to liberate it. And third, your intelligence is wrong. There are only forty-eight men in my party."

"Forty-eight, fifty-three—what is the difference?"

"Oh, there is a difference, Mr. Silva," said Roosevelt. He paused. "The other five are halfway to Nairobi by now."

"What do they propose to do once they get there?" asked Silva suspiciously.

"They propose to tell the American press that Teddy Roosevelt—who is, in all immodesty, the most popular and influential American of the past half century—is under military attack by the Belgian government. His brave little force is standing firm, but he can't hold out much longer without help, and if he should die while trying to free the citizens of the Congo from the yoke of Belgian tyranny, he wants America to know that he died at the hands of King Albert, who, I believe, has more than enough problems in Europe without adding this to his burden."

"You are mad!" exclaimed Silva. "Do you really think anyone will care what happens here?"

"That is probably just what the Mahdi said to Chinese Gordon at the fall of Khartoum," said Roosevelt easily. "Read your history books and you'll see what happened when the British people learned of his death."

"You are bluffing!"

"You are welcome to think so," replied Roosevelt calmly. "But in two months' time, fifty thousand Americans will be standing in line to fight at my side in the Congo—and if you kill me, you can multiply that number by one hundred, and most of them will want to take the battle right to Belgium."

"This is the most preposterous thing I have ever heard!" exclaimed Silva.

Roosevelt reached into a pocket of his hunting jacket and pulled out a thick, official-looking document he had written the previous day.

"It's all here in black and white, Mr. Silva. I suggest that you deliver it to your superior as quickly as possible, because he'll want to send it on to Belgium, and I know how long these things take." He paused. "We'd like you out of the Congo in six months, so you can see that there's no time to waste."

"We are going nowhere!"

Roosevelt sighed deeply. "I'm afraid you are up against an historic inevitability," he said. "You have twenty armed men. I have forty-seven, not counting myself. It would be suicidal for you to attack us here and now, and by the time you return from Stanleyville, I'll have a force of more than thirty thousand

Mangbetu plus a number of other tribes, who will not be denied their independence any longer."

"My men are a trained military force," said Silva. "Yours are a ragtag band of outcasts and poachers."

"But good shots," said Roosevelt with a confident grin. He paused again and the grin vanished. "Besides, if you succeed in killing me, you'll be the man who precipitated a war with the United States. Are you quite certain you want that responsibility?"

Silva was silent for a moment. Finally he spoke.

"I will return to Stanleyville," he announced. "But I will be back. This I promise you."

"We won't be here," answered Roosevelt.

"Where will you be?"

"I have no idea—but I have every intention of remaining alive until news of what's happening here gets back to America." Roosevelt paused and smiled. "The Congo is a large country, Mr. Silva. I plan to make many more friends here while awaiting Belgium's decision."

Silva got abruptly to his feet. "With this paper," he said, holding up the document, "you have signed not only your own death warrant, but the death warrant of every man who follows you."

Boyes laughed from his position halfway down the table. "Do you know how many death warrants have been issued on me? I'll just add this one to my collection." He paused, amused. "I've never had one written in French before."

"You are both mad!" snapped Silva, stalking off toward his men.

Roosevelt watched the assistant governor mount his horse and gallop off, followed by his twenty soldiers.

"I suppose we should have invited him to stay for dinner," he remarked pleasantly.

"You don't really think this is going to work, do you?" asked Boyes.

"Certainly."

"It's a lot of fancy talk, but it boils down to the fact that we're still only fifty-three men," said Boyes. "You'll never get the natives to go to war with the Belgians. They haven't any guns, and even if they did, we can't prepare them to fight a modern war in just six months' time."

"John, you know Africa and you know hunting," answered Roosevelt seriously, "but I know politics and I know history. The Congo is an embarrassment to the Belgians; Leopold wasted so much money here that his own government took it away from him two years ago. Furthermore, Europe is heading hell-for-leather for a war such as it has never seen before. The last thing they need is a battle with America over a piece of territory they didn't really want to begin with."

"They must want it or they wouldn't be here," said Boyes stubbornly.

Roosevelt shook his head. "They just didn't want anyone else to have it. When Africa was divided among the great powers in 1885, Belgium would have lost face if it hadn't insisted on its right to colonize the Congo, but it's been an expensive investment that has been both a financial drain and a political embarrassment for more than two decades." He paused. "And what I said about General Gordon was true. He refused to leave Khartoum, and his death eventually forced the British government to take over the Sudan when the public demanded that they avenge him." Suddenly Roosevelt grinned. "A lot more people voted for me than ever even heard of Gordon. Believe me, John, the Belgian government will bluster and threaten for a month or two, and then they'll start negotiating."

"Well, it all sounds logical," said Boyes. "But I still can't believe that a force of fifty-three men can take over an entire country. It's just not possible."

"Once and for all, John, we are *not* a force of fifty-three men," said Roosevelt. "We are a *potential* force of a million outraged Americans."

"So you keep saying. But still—"

"John, I trust you implicitly when we're stalking an elephant or a lion. Try to have an equal degree of trust in me when we're doing what *I* do best."

"I wish I could," said Boyes. "But it just *can't* be this easy."

On December 3, 1910, five months and twenty-seven days after receiving Roosevelt's demands, the Belgian government officially relinquished all claims to the Congo, and began withdrawing their nationals.

VIII

"*Damn that Taft!*"

Roosevelt crumpled the telegram, which had been delivered by runner from Stanleyville, in his massive hand and threw it to the ground. The sound of his angry, high-pitched voice combined with the violence of his gesture frightened a number of birds which had been searching for insects on the sprawling lawn, and they flew, squawking and screeching, to sanctuary in a cluster of nearby trees.

"Bad news, Mr. President?" asked Boyes.

They were staying at the house of M. Beauregard de Vincennes, a French plantation owner, some fifteen miles west of Stanleyville, on the shores of the Congo River. Three dozen of Roosevelt's men were camped out on the grounds, while the remainder were alternately hunting ivory and preparing the Lulua and Baluba, two of the major tribes in the area, for visits from Roosevelt himself.

"The man has no gratitude, no gratitude at all!" snapped Roosevelt. "I gave him the Presidency, handed it to him as a gift, and now I've offered to give him a foothold in Africa as well, and he has the unmitigated gall to tell me that he can't afford to send me the men and the money I've requested!"

"Is he sending anything at all?" asked Boyes.

"I requested ten thousand men, and he's sending six hundred!" said Roosevelt furiously. "I told him I needed at least twenty million dollars to build roads and extend the railroad from Uganda, and he's offering three million. Three million dollars for a country a third the size of the United States! *Damn* the man! J. P. Morgan may be a scoundrel and a brigand, but *he* would recognize an opportunity like this and pounce on it, I'll guarantee you that!" He paused and suddenly nodded his head vigorously. "By God, that's what I'll do! I'll wire Morgan this afternoon!"

"I thought he was your mortal enemy," remarked Boyes. "At least, that's the way it sounds whenever you mention him."

"Nonsense!" said Roosevelt. "We were on different sides of the political fence, but he's a competent man, which is more than I can say for the idiot sitting in the White House." Roosevelt grinned. "And he loves railroads. Yes, I'll wire him this afternoon."

"Are we refusing President Taft's offer, then?"

"Certainly not. We need all the manpower and money we can get. I'll wire our acceptance, and send off some telegrams to a few sympathetic newspaper publishers telling them what short shrift we're getting from Washington. I can't put any more pressure on Taft from here, but perhaps *they* can." Roosevelt shook his head sadly. "It serves me right for putting a fool in the White House. I tell you, John, if I didn't have a job to do right here, I'd go back to the States and take the nomination away from him in 1912. The man doesn't deserve to run a second time."

Roosevelt ranted against the "fat fool" in the White House for another fifteen minutes, then retired to his room to draft his telegrams. When he emerged an hour later for lunch, he was once again his usual pleasant, vigorous, optimistic self. Boyes, Bill Buckley, Mickey Norton, Yank Rogers, and Deaf Banks were sitting at a table beneath an ancient tree, and all of them except Banks, who hadn't heard the ex-President's approach, stood up as he joined them.

"Please be seated, gentlemen," said Roosevelt, pulling up a chair. "What's on the menu for this afternoon?"

"Salad and cold guinea hen in some kind of sauce," answered Norton. "Or that's what Madame Vincennes told me, anyway."

"I love guinea fowl," enthused Roosevelt. "That will be just bully!" He paused. "Good people, Monsieur and Madame Vincennes. I'm delighted that they offered to be our hosts." He paused. "This is much more pleasant than being cooped up in those airless little government buildings in Stanleyville."

"I hear we got some bad news from your pal Bill Taft," ventured Rogers.

"It's all taken care of," answered Roosevelt, confidently tapping the pocket that held his telegrams. "The men he's sending will arrive during the rainy season, anyway—and by the time the rains are over, we'll have more than enough manpower." He looked around the table. "It's time we considered some more immediate problems, gentlemen."

"What problems did you have in mind, sir?" asked Buckley, as six black servants approached the table, bearing trays of salads and drinks.

"We've had this country for two months now," answered Roosevelt. "It's time we began doing something with it—besides decimating its elephant population, that is," he added harshly.

"Well, we could decimate the Belgians that have stayed behind," said Buckley with an amused smile. "Billy Pickering would like that."

"I'm being serious, Mr. Buckley," said Roosevelt, taking a small crust of bread from his plate and tossing it to a nearby starling, which immediately picked it up and pranced off with it. "What's the purpose of making the Belgians leave if we don't improve the lot of the inhabitants? Everywhere we've gone we've promised to bring the benefits of democracy to the Congo. I think it's time we started delivering on that promise. The people deserve no less."

"Boy!" said Norton to one of the servants. "This coffee's cold. Go heat it up."

The servant nodded, bowed, put the coffee pot back on the tray, and walked toward the kitchen building.

"I don't know how you're going to civilize them when they can't remember from one day to the next that coffee's supposed to be served hot and not warm," said Norton. "And look at the way he's loafing: it could be hot when he gets it and cold by the time he brings it here."

"The natives don't drink coffee, so it can hardly be considered important to them," answered Roosevelt.

"They don't vote, or hold trial by jury, either," offered Buckley.

"Well, if we're to introduce them to the amenities of civilization, I think that voting and jury trials come well ahead of coffee drinking, Mr. Buckley."

"They can't even read," said Buckley. "How are you going to teach them to vote?"

"I plan to set up a public school system throughout the country," said Roosevelt. "The Belgian missionaries made a start, but they were undermanned and under-financed. In my pocket is a telegram that will appear in more than a thousand American newspapers, an open appeal to teachers and missionaries to come to the Congo and help educate the populace."

"That could take years, sir," noted Boyes.

"Ten at the most," answered Roosevelt confidently.

"How will you pay 'em, Teddy?" asked Rogers. "Hell, you can't even pay *us.*"

"The missionaries will be paid by their churches, of course," said Roosevelt. "As for the teachers, I suppose we'll have to pay them with land initially."

"That might not sit too well with the people whose land we're giving away," noted Rogers.

"Yank, if there's one thing the Congo abounds in, besides insects and humidity, it's land."

"You say it'll take ten years to educate them," continued Rogers. "How will you hold elections in the meantime?"

"By voice," answered Roosevelt. "Every man and woman will enter the polling place and state his or her preference. As a matter of fact, there will probably be a lot less vote fraud that way."

"Did I hear you say that women are going to vote too, Teddy?" asked Yank Rogers.

"They're citizens of the Congo, aren't they?"

"But they don't even vote back home!"

"That's going to change," said Roosevelt firmly. "Our founding fathers were wrong not to give women the right to vote, and there's no reason to make the same mistake here. They're human beings, the same as us, and they deserve the same rights and privileges." Suddenly he grinned. "I pity the man who has to tell my Alice that she can't cast her vote at the polls. There won't be enough of him left to bury!"

"You know, we could raise money with a hut tax," suggested Buckley. "That's what the British have done wherever they've had an African colony."

"A hut tax?" asked Roosevelt.

Buckley nodded. "Tax every native ten or twenty shillings a year for each hut he erects. It not only raises money for the treasury, but it forces them to be something more than subsistence farmers, since they need money to pay the tax."

Roosevelt shook his head adamantly. "We're supposed to be freeing them, Mr. Buckley, not enslaving them."

"Besides," added Boyes, "it never worked that well in British East. If they didn't pay their hut tax, the government threw them into jail." He turned to Roosevelt and smiled. "You know what the Kikuyu and Wakamba called the jail in Nairobi? The King Georgi Hoteli. It was the only place they knew of where they could get three square meals a day and a free roof over their heads." He chuckled at the memory. "Once word of it got out, they were lining up to get thrown in jail."

"Well, there will be no such attempt to exploit the natives of the Congo," said Roosevelt. "We must always remember that this is *their* country and that our duty is to teach them the ways of democracy."

"That may be easier said than done," said Rogers.

"Why should you think so, Yank?" asked Roosevelt.

"Democracy's a pretty alien concept to them," answered Rogers. "It's going to take some getting used to."

"It was an alien concept to young Booker T. Washington and George Washington Carver, too," said Roosevelt, "but they seem to have adapted to it readily enough. It's never difficult to get used to freedom."

"We ain't talking freedom, Teddy," said Rogers. "They were free for thousands of years before the Belgians showed up, but they ain't never had a democracy. Their tribes are ruled by chiefs and witch doctors, not congressmen."

"And now that the Belgians are clearing out," added Norton, "our biggest problem is going to be to stop them from killing each other long enough to get to the polls."

"All of you keep predicting the most dire consequences," said Roosevelt irritably, "and yet you ignore the enormous strides the American Negro has taken since the Emancipation Proclamation. I tell you, gentlemen, that freedom has no color and democracy is not the special province of one race."

Boyes smiled, and Buckley turned to him.

"What are you looking so amused about, John?

You've been here long enough to know everything we've said is the truth."

"You all think you're discouraging Mr. Roosevelt, and that if you tell him enough stories about how savage the natives are, maybe you'll convince him to join you long enough to kill every last elephant in the Congo and then go back to Nairobi." Boyes paused. "But I know him a little better than you do, and if there's one thing he can't resist, it's a challenge." He turned to Roosevelt. "Am I right, sir?"

Roosevelt grinned back at him. "Absolutely, Mr. Boyes." He looked around at his companions. "Gentlemen," he announced, "I've heard enough doomsaying for one day. It's time to roll up our sleeves and get to work."

IX

Roosevelt stared at his image in the full-length ornate gilt mirror that adorned the parlor of the state house at Stanleyville, and adjusted the tie of his morning suit.

"Good thing that little German tailor decided not to leave," he remarked to Boyes, who was similarly clad, "or we'd be conducting matters of state in our safari clothes."

"I'd be a damned sight more comfortable in them," replied Boyes, checking his appearance in the mirror, and deciding that his hair needed more combing.

"Nonsense, John," said Roosevelt. "We've got reporters and photographers from all over the world here."

"Personally, I'd much rather face a charging elephant," said Boyes, looking out the window. "I don't like crowds."

Roosevelt smiled. "I'd forgotten just how much I *miss* them." He put on his top hat and walked to the door. "Well, we might as well begin."

Boyes, unhappy and uncomfortable, and feeling quite naked without his pistol and rifle, followed the American out the front door to the raised wooden platform that had been constructed in front of the state house the previous day. The press was there, as Roosevelt had said: reporters and photographers from America, Belgium, England, France, Italy, Portugal, Kenya, and even a pair of Orientals had made the long, arduous trek to Stanleyville to hear this speech and record the moment for posterity. Seated on the front row of chairs, in a section reserved for VIPs and dignitaries, were the paramount chiefs of the Mangbetu, the Simba, the Mongo, the Luba, the Bwaka, the Zande, and the Kongo (which centuries ago had given the country its name). There was even a pair of pygmy chiefs, one of whom was completely naked except for a loincloth, a pair of earrings, and a necklace made of leopards' claws, while the other wore a suit that could have been tailored on Savile Row.

The crowd, some six hundred strong, and divided almost equally between whites and black Africans, immediately ceased its chattering when Roosevelt mounted the platform and waited in polite expectation while he walked to a podium and pulled some notes out of his pocket.

"Good morning, ladies and gentlemen. I thank you for your attendance and patience. I realize that, with our transportation system not yet constructed, you may have had some slight difficulty in reaching Stanleyville"—he paused for the good-natured laughter that he knew would follow—"but you're here now, and we're delighted to have you as the guests of our new nation."

He paused, pulled a brand-new handkerchief out of his pocket, and wiped away the sweat that had begun pouring down his face.

"We are here to proclaim the sovereignty of this beautiful land. Some years ago it was known as the Congo Free State. At the time, that was a misnomer, for it was anything but free. Today it is no longer a misnomer, and so it shall once again be known as the Congo Free State, an independent nation dedicated to the preservation of human dignity and the celebration of human endeavor."

A pair of blue touracos began shrieking in a nearby tree, and he smiled and waited a few seconds until the noise had subsided.

"What's past is past," he continued, "and the Congo Free State begins life with a clean slate. It bears no rancor toward any person or any nation that may have exploited its resources and its people in the past. But"—and here Roosevelt's chin jutted out pugnaciously—"this land will never be plundered or exploited again." He stared darkly out at his audience. "Never again will a privileged minority impose its will upon the majority. Never again will one tribe bear arms against another. Never again will women do most of the work and reap none of the benefits. And never again will the dreadful spectres of ignorance, poverty, and disease run rampant in what Henry Stanley termed Darkest Africa." He raised his voice dramatically. "From this day forward, we shall illuminate the Congo Free State with the light of democracy, and turn it into the exemplar of Brightest Africa!"

Roosevelt paused long enough for his words to be translated, then smiled and nodded as the row of chiefs rose to their feet and cheered wildly, followed, somewhat less enthusiastically, by the Europeans.

"Thank you, my friends," he continued when the chiefs finally sat down. "We who have been fortunate enough to help in the birth of the Congo Free State have great plans for its future." He smiled triumphantly. "Great plans, indeed!" he repeated emphatically.

"Within two years, we will extend the East African Railway from its present terminus in Uganda all the way to Stanleyville, and within another year to Leopoldville. This will give us access to the Indian Ocean, as the Congo River gives us access to the Atlantic, and with the modern farming methods we plan to introduce, we will shortly be shipping exports in great quantity to both coasts."

There was more applause, a little less rabid this time, as most of the chiefs had only the haziest understanding of an economy that extended beyond their own tribes.

"We will construct public schools throughout the country," Roosevelt added. "Our goal is nothing less than one-hundred-percent literacy by the year 1930."

This time the applause came only from the chiefs, as the whites in the audience looked openly skeptical.

"We will soon begin the construction of modern hospitals in every major city in the Congo Free

State," continued Roosevelt, "and no citizen shall ever again want for medical care. American engineers will build dams the length of the Congo River, so that we can generate all the electricity that a modern nation will need. While leaving vast tracts of land untouched as national parks and game reserves, we will nonetheless crisscross the country with a network of roads, so that no village, no matter how remote, remains inaccessible."

He paused and glared at the disbelieving white faces in his audience.

"We will do everything I have said," he concluded. "And we will do it sooner than you think!"

The assembled chiefs began cheering and jumping around in their enthusiasm, and the remainder of the audience, sensing that he had concluded the major part of his address, applauded politely.

"And now, ladies and gentlemen, if you will all rise, we will, for the very first time, raise the flag of the Congo Free State." He turned to Boyes. "Mr. Boyes?"

Boyes withdrew the folded flag that he had been carrying inside his morning coat, waited for an honor guard of khaki-clad native soldiers to approach, and solemnly handed the flag over to their leader. The soldiers then marched to a recently-erected flagpole near the platform, and began raising a banner that depicted the colorful shields of twenty of the major tribes arranged in a pattern on a field of green, while Yank Rogers, who had been unable to create a national anthem on two days' notice, played a military march on his ancient bugle. Roosevelt stood at attention and saluted, Boyes and the chiefs followed suit, and the reporters, politicians, and dignitaries were quick to rise to their feet as well.

When the flag had been raised and the rope secured at the base of the flagpole, Roosevelt faced the crowd once more.

"I have been selected, by the unanimous consent of the tribes that are represented here today, to draft and implement a democratic constitution for the Congo Free State. During this time I shall hold the office of Chief Administrator, an office that will be abolished when the first national election is held one year from today. At that time all the people of the Congo Free State, regardless of race or gender, will choose their own President and legislature, and their destiny will finally be in their own hands."

He stared out at the audience.

"I thank you for your attendance at this historic ceremony. Lunch will be provided for everyone on the lawn, and I will be available for interviews throughout the afternoon."

He climbed down from the platform to one last round of applause, finally allowed them a look at the famed Roosevelt grin, waited for Boyes to join him, and disappeared into the interior of the state house.

"How was I, John?" he asked anxiously.

"I thought you were excellent, Mr. President," answered Boyes truthfully.

"Mr. Chief Administrator, you mean," Roosevelt corrected him. Suddenly he smiled. "Although by this time you certainly know me well enough to call me Teddy. Everyone else does."

"I think I prefer Mr. President," replied Boyes. "I'm used to it."

Roosevelt shrugged, then looked out the window

as the crowd began lining up at the long buffet tables.

"They don't think I can do it, do they, John?"

"No, sir, they don't," answered Boyes honestly.

"Well, they'd be correct if I applied their outmoded methods," said Roosevelt. He drew himself up to his full height. "However, this is a new century. We have new technologies, new methods, and new outlooks."

"But this is an old country," said Boyes.

"What is that supposed to mean, John?"

"Just that it might not be ready for your new approach, Mr. President."

"You saw the chiefs out there, John," said Roosevelt. "They're my strongest supporters."

"It's in their best interest to be," said Boyes. "After all, you've promised them the moon."

"And I'll deliver it," said Roosevelt resolutely.

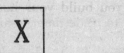

X

Boyes walked into the state house and was ushered into Roosevelt's office.

"Where have you been, John?" asked Roosevelt. "I expected you back three days ago."

"It took a little longer than I thought to set up my trading company," answered Boyes. "But if your laborers ever arrive, at least they won't starve to death. I've got commitments for flour and meat."

"What are you trading for them?"

"Iodine," answered Boyes. "That's what took me so long. My shipment was late arriving from Nairobi."

"Iodine?" repeated Roosevelt, curious.

Boyes smiled. "There are some infections even a witch doctor can't cure." He sat down in a leather chair opposite Roosevelt's desk, looking quite pleased with himself. "An ounce of iodine for thirty pounds of flour or one hundred pounds of meat."

"That's immoral, John. These people *need* that medication."

"Our people will need that food," answered Boyes.

"My hospitals will put you out of business," said Roosevelt sternly. "We will never withhold treatment despite a patient's inability to pay for it."

"When you build your hospitals, I'll find something else to trade them," said Boyes with a shrug. He decided to change the subject. "I hear you held your first local election while I was gone. How did it go?"

"I would call it a limited success."

"Oh?"

"It was a trial run, so to speak," said Roosevelt. "We selected a district at random and tried to show them how an election works." He paused. "We had a turnout of almost ninety percent, which is certainly very promising."

"Let me guess about the unpromising part," said Boyes. "Your candidates didn't get a single cross-over vote."

Roosevelt nodded his head grimly. "The vote went one hundred percent along tribal lines."

"I hope you're not surprised."

"No, but I *am* disappointed." Roosevelt sighed. "I'll simply have to keep explaining to them that they are supposed to vote on the issues and not on tribal connections until they finally understand the principle involved."

For the first time since they had met, Boyes felt sorry for the American.

* * *

"Not guilty?" repeated Roosevelt. "How in the name of pluperfect hell could they come in with a verdict of not guilty?"

He had turned the local theater into a courtroom, and had spent the better part of a week instructing the members of the Luba and Zande tribes in the intricacies of the jury system. Then he himself had acted as the presiding judge at the Congo Free State's very first trial by jury, and he was now in his make-shift chambers, barely able to control his fury.

"It was a unanimous decision," said Charlie Ross, who had acted as bailiff.

"I know it was a unanimous decision, Mr. Ross!" thundered Roosevelt. "What I don't know is how, in the face of all the evidence, they could come up with it?"

"Why don't you ask them?" suggested Ross.

"By God, that's exactly what I'll do!" said Roosevelt. "Bring them in here, one at a time."

Ross left the room for about five minutes, during which time Roosevelt tried unsuccessfully to compose himself.

"Sir," said Ross, re-entering in the company of a tall, slender black man, "this is Tambika, one of the jurors."

"Thank you, Mr. Ross," said Roosevelt. He turned to the African. "Mr. Tambika," he said in heavily-accented Swahili, "I wonder if you could explain your decision to me."

"Explain it, King Teddy?" asked Tambika, bewildered.

"Please call me Mr. Chief Administrator," said Roosevelt uncomfortably. He paused. "The man, Toma, was accused of stealing six cows. Four eyewitnesses claimed to see him driving the cows back toward his own home, and Mr. Kalimi showed you a bill of sale he received when he purchased the cows from Toma. There is no question that the cows bore the mark, or brand, of the plaintiff, Mr. Salamaki. Can you please tell me why you found him innocent?"

"Ah, now I understand," said Tambika with a large smile. "Toma owes me money. How can he pay me if he is in jail?"

"But he broke the law."

"True," agreed Tambika.

"Then you must find him guilty."

"But if I had found him guilty, he would never be able to pay me what he owes me," protested Tambika. "That is not justice, King Teddy."

Roosevelt argued with Tambika for another few minutes, then dismissed him and had Ross bring in the next juror, an old man named Begoni. After reciting the evidence again, he put the question to the old man.

"It is very clear," answered Begoni. "Toma is a Luba, as am I. Salamaki is a Zande. It is impossible for the Luba to commit a crime against the Zande."

"But that is precisely what he did, Mr. Begoni," said Roosevelt.

The old man shook his head. "The Zande have been stealing our cattle and our women since God created the world. It is our right to steal them back."

"The law says otherwise," Roosevelt pointed out.

"Whose law?" asked the old man, staring at him with no show of fear or awe. "Yours or God's?"

"If Mr. Toma were a Zande, would you have found him guilty?"

"Certainly," answered Begoni, as if the question were too ridiculous to consider.

"If Mr. Toma were a Zande and you knew for a fact that he had *not* stolen the cattle, would you have found him innocent?" asked Roosevelt.

"No."

"Why?" asked Roosevelt in exasperation.

"There are too many Zande in the world."

"That will be all, Mr. Begoni."

"Thank you, Mr. Teddy," said the old man, walking to the door. He paused for a moment just before leaving. "I like jury trials," he announced. "It saves much bloodshed."

"I can't believe it!" said Roosevelt, getting to his feet and stalking back and forth across the room after the door had closed behind Begoni. "I spent an entire week with these people, explaining how the system works!"

"Are you ready for the next one, sir?" asked Ross.

"No!" snapped Roosevelt. "I already know what he'll say. Toma's a tribal brother. Toma can't pay the bride price for his daughter if we throw him in jail. If a document, such as a bill of sale, implicates a Luba, then it must have been cursed by a Zande witch doctor and cannot be believed." Roosevelt stopped and turned to Ross. "What is the matter with these people, Charlie? Don't they understand what I'm trying to do for them?"

"They have their own system of justice, Mr. President," answered Ross gently.

"I've seen that system in action," said Roosevelt contemptuously. "A witch doctor touches a hot iron to the accused's tongue. If he cries out, he's guilty;

if he doesn't, he's innocent. What kind of system is that, I ask you?"

"One they believe in," said Ross.

"Well, that's that," said Roosevelt grimly, after opening the weekly mail. "Morgan isn't interested in investing in a railroad."

"Is there anyone else you can ask?" inquired Boyes.

"Bill Taft is mismanaging the economy. I have a feeling that the people who can afford to invest are feeling exceptionally conservative this year."

Nevertheless, he wrote another thirty letters that afternoon, each soliciting funds, and mailed them the next morning. He expressed great confidence that the money would soon be forthcoming, but he began making contingency plans for the day, not far off, when construction of the Trans-Congo Railway would be forced to come to a halt.

"What do you mean, you have no more supplies?" demanded Roosevelt. "You had ample track for another five miles, Mr. Brody."

Brody, a burly American, stood uncomfortably before Roosevelt's desk, fidgeting with his pith helmet, which he held awkwardly in his huge hands.

"Yes, we did, Mr. Roosevelt."

"Well?"

"It's the natives, sir," said Brody. "They keep stealing it."

"Rubbish! What possible use could they have for steel track?"

"You wouldn't believe the uses they put it to, sir," answered Brody. "They use it to support their huts, and to make pens for their goats and cattle, and they melt it down for spearheads."

"Well, then, take it back."

"We were expressly instructed not to harm any of the natives, sir, and whenever we've tried to retrieve our tracks we've been threatened with spears, and occasionally even guns. If we can't take them back by force, they're going to stay right where they are until they rust."

"Who's the headman in your area, Mr. Brody?" asked Roosevelt.

"A Mangbetu named Matapoli."

"I know him personally," said Roosevelt, his expression brightening. "Bring him here and perhaps we can get this situation resolved."

"That could take six weeks, sir—and that's assuming he'll come with me."

Roosevelt shook his head. "That won't do, Mr. Brody. I can't pay your men to sit on their hands for six weeks." He paused, then nodded to himself, his decision made. "I'll return with you. It's time I got out among the people again, anyway."

He summoned Yank Rogers while Brody was getting lunch at a small restaurant down the street.

"What can I do for you, Teddy?" asked the American.

"I'm going to have to go to Mangbetu country, Yank," answered Roosevelt. "I want you and Mr. Buckley to remain in Stanleyville and keep an eye on things here while I'm gone."

"What about Boyes?" asked Rogers. "Isn't that his job?"

"John will be accompanying me," answered Roosevelt. "The Mangbetu seem to be very fond of him."

"They're equally fond of you, Teddy."

"I enjoy his company," said Roosevelt. He smiled wryly. "I'll also find it comforting to know that the state house hasn't been sold to the highest bidder in my absence.

"John," remarked Roosevelt, as he and Boyes sat beside a campfire, "have you noticed that we haven't seen any elephant sign in more than a week now?"

The horses started whinnying as the wind brought the scent of lion and hyena to them.

"Perhaps they've migrated to the west," said Boyes.

"Come on, John," said Roosevelt. "I'm not as old a hand at this as you are, but I know when an area's been shot out."

"We've shipped a lot of ivory to Mombasa and Zanzibar during the past year," said Boyes.

"I didn't mind our men making a little money on the side, John, but I won't have them decimating the herds."

"They've been more than a year without a paycheck," answered Boyes seriously. "If you tell them they have to stop hunting ivory, I doubt that more than a dozen of them will stay in the Congo."

"Then we'll have to make do without their services," said Roosevelt. "The elephants belong to the people of the Congo Free State now. We've got to start a game department and charge for hunting licenses while there's still something left to hunt."

"If you say so," replied Boyes.

Roosevelt stared long and hard at him. "Will *you* be one of the ones who leaves, John?"

Boyes shook his head. "I'm the one who talked you

into this in the first place, Mr. President," he answered. "I'll stay as long as you do." He paused thoughtfully. "I've made more than my share of money off the ivory anyway, and I suppose we really ought to stop while there are still some elephants left. I was just pointing out the consequences of abolishing poaching."

"Then start passing the word as soon as we get back," said Roosevelt. Suddenly he frowned. "That's funny."

"What is, sir?"

"I felt very dizzy for just a moment there." He shrugged. "I'm sure it will pass."

But it didn't, and that night the ex-President came down with malaria. Boyes tended to him and nursed him back to health, but another week had been wasted, and Roosevelt had the distinct feeling that he didn't have too many of them left to put the country on the right track.

"Ah, my friend Johnny—and King Teddy!" Matapoli greeted them with a huge smile of welcome. "You honor my village with your presence."

"Your village has changed since the last time we were here," noted Boyes wryly.

Matapoli pointed proudly to the five railroad coach cars that his men had dragged miles through the bush over a period of months, and which now housed his immediate family and the families of four of the tribe's elders.

"Oh, yes," he said happily. "King Teddy promised us democracy, and he kept his promise." He pointed to one of the cars. "*My* democracy is the finest of all. Come join me inside it."

Roosevelt and Boyes exchanged ironic glances and followed Matapoli into the coach car, with was filled with some twenty or so of his children.

"King Teddy has returned!" enthused the Mangbetu chief. "We must have a hunt in the forest and have a feast in your honor."

"That's very thoughtful of you, Matapoli," said Roosevelt. "But it has been many months since we last saw each other. Let us talk together first."

"Yes, that would be very good," agreed Matapoli, puffing out his chest as the children recognized the two visitors and raced off to inform the rest of the village.

"Just how many children do you have?" asked Roosevelt.

Matapoli paused in thought for a moment. "Ten, and ten more, and then seven," he answered.

"And how many wives?"

"Five."

The puritanical American tried without success to hide his disapproval. "That's a very large family, Matapoli."

"Should be more, should be more," admitted the Mangbetu. "But it took many months to bring the democracies here."

"Had you left them on the track, you could have traveled all across the country on them," Boyes pointed out.

Matapoli threw back his head and laughed. "Why should I want to go to Lulua or Bwaka country?" he asked. "They would just kill me and take my democracies for themselves."

"Please try to understand, Matapoli," said Roosevelt. "There are no longer Mangbetu or Lulua or

Bwaka countries. There is just the Congo Free State, and you all live in it."

"You are king of all the countries, King Teddy," answered Matapoli. "You need have no fear. If the Bwaka say that you are not, then we shall kill them."

Roosevelt spent the next ten minutes trying to explain the Congo Free State to Matapoli, who was no closer to comprehending it at the end of the discussion than at the beginning.

"All right," said the American with a sigh of resignation. "Let's get back to talking about the trains."

"Trains?" repeated Matapoli.

"The democracies, and the steel logs they rolled upon," interjected Boyes.

"Another gift from King Teddy," said Matapoli enthusiastically. "No longer can the leopards and the hyenas break through the thorns and kill my cattle. Now I use the metal thorns, and my animals are safe."

"The metal thorns were built so that you and the other Mangbetu could travel many miles without having to walk," said Roosevelt.

"Why should we wish to go many miles?" asked Matapoli, honestly puzzled. "The river runs beside the village, and the forest and its game are just a short walk away."

"You might wish to visit another tribe."

Matapoli smiled. "How could we sneak up on our enemies in the democracies? They are too large, and they would make too much noise when they rolled upon the iron thorns." He shook his head. "No, King Teddy, they are much better right here, where we can put them to use."

Long after the feast was over and Roosevelt and

Boyes were riding their horses back toward Stanleyville, Roosevelt, who had been replaying the frus-
trating day over and over in his mind, finally sighed
and muttered: "By God, that probably *is* the best use
they could have been put to!"

Boyes found the remark highly amusing, and burst
into laughter. A moment later Roosevelt joined him
with a hearty laugh of his own, and that was the
official end of the Trans-Congo Railway.

They came to a newly-paved road when they were
fifteen miles out of Stanleyville and, glad to finally
be free of the bush and the forest, they veered their
mounts onto it. As they continued their journey, they
passed dozens of men and women walking alongside
the road.

"Why don't they walk *on* it, John?" asked Roosevelt curiously. "There can't be fifteen trucks in the
whole of the Congo. Until we import some more, we
might as well put the roads to some use."

"They're barefoot," Boyes pointed out.

"So what? The road is a lot smoother than the
rocks alongside it."

"It's also a lot hotter," answered Boyes. "By high
noon you could fry an egg on it."

"You mean we've spent a million dollars on roads
for which there not only aren't any cars and trucks,
but that the people can't even walk on?"

"This isn't America, sir."

"A point that is being driven home daily," muttered Roosevelt wearily.

XI

ROOSEVELT SAT AT HIS DESK, STARING AT A NUMBER OF letters and documents that lay stacked neatly in front of him. To his left was a photograph of Edith and his children, to his right a picture of himself delivering a State of the Union address to the United States Congress, and behind him, on an ornate brass stand, was the flag of the Congo Free State.

Finally, with a sigh, he opened the final letter, read it quickly, and, frowning, placed it atop the stack.

"Bad news, Mr. President?" asked Boyes, who was sitting in the leather chair on the opposite side of the desk.

"No worse than the rest of them," answered Roosevelt. "That was from Mr. Bennigan, our chief engineer on the Stanley Falls Bridge. He sends his regrets, but his men haven't been paid in three weeks, and he's going to have to pull out." He stared at the letter. "There's no postmark, of course, but I would guess that it took at least two weeks to get here."

"We didn't need him anyway," said Boyes, dismissing the matter with a shrug. "What's the sense of building a bridge over the falls if we don't have any trains or cars?"

"Because someday we'll have them, John, and when we do, they're going to need roads and tracks and bridges."

"When that happy day arrives, I'm sure we'll have enough money to complete work on the bridge," replied Boyes.

Roosevelt sighed. "It's not as devastating a blow as losing the teachers. How many of them have left?"

"Just about all."

"Damn!" muttered Roosevelt. "How can we educate the populace if there's no one to teach them?"

"With all due respect, sir, they don't need Western educations," said Boyes. "You're trying to turn them into Americans, and they're not. Reading and writing are no more important to them than railroads are."

Roosevelt stared at him for a long moment. "What do *you* think is important to them, John?"

"You're talking about a primitive society," answered Boyes. "They need to learn crop rotation and hygiene and basic medicine far more than they need roads that they'll never use and railroad cars that they think are simply huts on wheels."

"You're wrong, John," said Roosevelt adamantly. "A little black African baby is no different than a little black American baby—or a little white American baby, for that matter. If we can get them young enough, and educate them thoroughly enough . . ."

"I don't like to contradict you, sir," interrupted Boyes, "but you're wrong. What's the point of having ten thousand college graduates if they all have to go home to their huts every night because there aren't two hundred jobs for educated men in the whole country? If you want to have a revolution on your hands, raise their expectations, prepare them to live and function in London or New York—and then make them stay in the Congo."

Roosevelt shook his head vigorously. "If we did things your way, these people would stay in ignorance and poverty forever. I told you when we began this enterprise that I wasn't coming here to turn the Congo into my private hunting preserve." He paused. "I haven't found the key yet, but if anyone can bring the Congo into the twentieth century, I can."

"Has it occurred to you that perhaps no one can?" suggested Boyes gently.

"Not for a moment," responded Roosevelt firmly.

"I'll stay as long as you do, sir," said Boyes. "You know that. But if you don't come up with some answers pretty soon, we may be the last two white men in this country, except for the missionaries and some of the Belgian planters who stayed behind. Almost half our original party has already left."

"They were just here for ivory or adventure," said Roosevelt dismissively. "We need people who care about this country more than we need people who are here merely to plunder it." Suddenly he stared out the window at some fixed point in space.

"Are you all right, sir?" asked Boyes after Roosevelt had remained motionless for almost a minute.

"Never better," answered the American suddenly. "You know, John, I see now that I've been going about this the wrong way. No one cares as much for the future of the Congo as the people themselves. I was wrong to try to bring in help from outside; in the long run, any progress we make here will be much more meaningful if it's accomplished by our own efforts."

"Ours?" repeated Boyes, puzzled. "You mean yours and mine?"

"I mean the citizens of the Congo Free State," answered Roosevelt. "I've been telling you and the engineers and the teachers and the missionaries what they need. I think it's about time I told the people and rallied them to their own cause."

"We've already promised them democracy," said Boyes. "And there's at least one Mangbetu village that will swear we delivered it to them," he added with a smile.

"Those were politicians' promises, designed to get our foot in the door," said Roosevelt. "Democracy may be a right, but it isn't a gift. It requires effort and sacrifice. They've got to understand that."

"First they've got to understand what democracy means."

"They will, once I've explained it to them," answered Roosevelt.

"You mean in person?" asked Boyes.

"That's right," said Roosevelt. "I'll start in the eastern section of the country, now that my Swahili has become fluent, and as I move west I'll use translators. But I'm going to go out among the people myself. I'm certainly not doing any good sitting here in Stanleyville; it's time to go out on the stump and get my message across to the only people who really need to understand it." He paused. "I'd love to have your company, John, but there are so few of us left that I think it would be better for you to remain here and keep an eye on things."

"Whatever you say, Mr. President," replied Boyes. "When will you leave?"

"Tomorrow," said Roosevelt. He paused. "No. This afternoon. There's nothing more important to do, and we've no time to waste."

He went among the people for five weeks, and everywhere he stopped, the drums had anticipated his arrival and the tribes flocked to see him.

He took his time, avoided any hint of jingoism, and carefully explained the principles of democracy to them. He pointed out the necessity of education, the importance of modern farming methods, the need to end all forms of tribalism, and the advantages of a monied economy. At the end of each "town meeting," as he called them, he held a prolonged question-and-answer session, and then he moved on to the next major village and repeated the entire procedure again.

During the morning of his thirty-sixth day on the stump, he was joined by Yank Rogers, who rode down from Stanleyville to see him.

"Hello, Yank!" cried Roosevelt enthusiastically as he saw the American riding up to his tent, which had been pitched just outside of a Lulua village.

"Hi, Teddy," said Rogers, pulling up his horse and dismounting. "You're looking good. Getting out in the bush seems to agree with you."

"I feel as fit as a bull moose," replied Roosevelt with a smile. "How's John doing?"

"Getting rich, as usual," said Rogers, not without a hint of admiration for the enterprising Yorkshireman. "I thought he was going to be stuck with about a million pounds of flour when all the construction people pulled out, but he heard that there was a famine in Portuguese Angola, so he traded the flour for ivory, and then had Buckley and the Brittlebanks brothers cart it to Mombasa when they decided to call it quits, in exchange for half the profits."

"That sounds like John, all right," agreed Roosevelt. "I'm sorry to hear that we've lost Buckley and the others, though."

Rogers shrugged. "They're just Brits. What the hell do they know about democracy? They'd slit your throat in two seconds flat if someone told them that it would get 'em an audience with the King." He paused. "All except Boyes, anyway. He'd find some way to put the King on display and charge money for it."

Roosevelt chuckled heartily. "You know, I do believe you're right."

"So much for Mr. Boyes," said Rogers, "How's your campaign going?"

"Just bully," answered Roosevelt. "The response has been wildly enthusiastic." He paused. "I'm surprised news of it hasn't reached you."

"How could it?" asked Rogers. "There aren't any newspapers—and even if there were, these people speak three hundred different languages and none of 'em can read or write."

"Still," said Roosevelt, "I've made a start."

"I don't doubt it, sir."

"I'm drawing almost five hundred natives a day," continued Roosevelt. "That's more than fifteen thousand converts in just over a month."

"If they stay converted."

"They will."

"Just another six million to go," said Rogers with a chuckle.

"I'm sure they're passing the word."

"To their fellow tribesmen, maybe," answered Rogers. "I wouldn't bet on their talking to anyone else."

"You sound like a pessimist, Yank," said Roosevelt.

"Pessimism and realism are next-door neighbors on this continent, Teddy," said Rogers.

"And yet you stay," noted Roosevelt.

Rogers smiled. "I figure if anyone can whip this country into shape, it's you—and if you do, I want to be able to laugh at all those Brits who gave up and left."

"Well, stick around," said Roosevelt. "I'm just getting warmed up."

"Sounds like fun," said Rogers. "I haven't heard you rile up a crowd since you ran for Governor of New York. I was in Africa before you ran for President." Suddenly he reached into his shirt pocket and withdrew an envelope. "I almost forgot why I rode all this way," he said, handing it to Roosevelt.

"What is it?"

"A letter from Boyes," answered Rogers. "He said to deliver it to you personally."

Roosevelt opened the letter, read it twice, then crumpled it into a ball and stuffed it into a pocket.

"I'm afraid you're not going to be able to hear me

giving any speeches this week, Yank," he announced. "I've got to return to Stanleyville."

"Something wrong?"

Roosevelt nodded. "It seems that Billy Pickering found four Belgian soldiers in a remote area in the southwest, men who had never received word that the Belgians had withdrawn from the Congo, and shot them dead."

"You mean he had me ride all the way here just for that?" demanded Rogers.

"It's a matter of vital importance, Yank."

"What's so important about four dead men?" asked Rogers. "Life is cheap in Africa."

"The Belgian government is demanding reparation."

"Yeah, I see where *that* can make it a little more expensive," admitted Rogers.

XII

"I WASN'T SURE HOW YOU WANTED TO HANDLE IT," BOYES said, staring across the desk at Roosevelt, who had just returned to Stanleyville less than an hour before.

"You were right to summon me, John."

"So far they haven't made any threats, but we're receiving diplomatic communiqués every other day."

"What's the gist of them?"

"Reparation, as I mentioned in my note to you."

Roosevelt shook his head. "They know we don't have any money," he answered. "They want something else."

"Pickering's head on a platter, I should think," suggested Boyes.

"They don't care any more about their soldiers than *he* did," said Roosevelt. "Let me see those communiqués."

Boyes handed over a sheaf of papers, and Roosevelt spent the next few minutes reading through them.

"Well?" asked Boyes when the American had set the papers down.

"I don't have sufficient information," answered Roosevelt. "Have they gone to the world press with this?"

"If they have, we won't know it for months," said Boyes. "The most recent paper I've seen is a ten-week-old copy of the *East African Standard*." He paused. "Why would going to the press make a difference?"

"Because if they've gone public, then they're positioning themselves to try to take the Congo back from us, by proving that we can't protect European nationals."

"But they weren't nationals," said Boyes. "They were soldiers."

"That just makes our position worse," replied Roosevelt. "If we can't protect a group of armed men who know the Congo, how can we protect anyone else?"

"Then what do you want to do about Pickering?" inquired Boyes.

"Where is he now?"

"In the jail at Leopoldville. Charlie Ross brought him in dead drunk, and locked him away."

"The proper decision," said Roosevelt, nodding approvingly. "I must remember to commend him for it."

"I'm afraid you won't be able to, Mr. President," said Boyes. "He's back in Kenya."

"Charlie?" said Roosevelt, surprised. "I'd have thought he'd be just about the last one to leave."

Boyes paused and stared uncomfortably across the desk at Roosevelt.

"Except for Yank Rogers and me, he was."

"They're *all* gone?"

"Yes, sir." Boyes cleared his throat and continued: "You did your best, sir, but everything's coming unraveled. Most of them stuck it out for better than two years, but we always knew that sooner or later they'd leave. They're not bureaucrats and administrators, they're hunters and adventurers."

"I know, John," said Roosevelt, suddenly feeling his years. "And I don't hold it against them. They helped us more than we had any right to expect." He paused and sighed deeply. "I had rather hoped we'd have a bureaucracy in place by this time."

"I know, sir."

"I wonder if it would have done much good," Roosevelt mused aloud. He looked across at Boyes. "That trip I just returned from—I wasted my time, didn't I?"

"Yes, sir, you did."

"We needed more teachers," said Roosevelt. "One man can't educate them overnight. We needed more teachers, and more money, and more time."

Boyes shook his head. "You needed a different country, Mr. President."

"Let's have no more talk about the inferiority of the African race, John," said Roosevelt. "I'm not up to it today."

"I've never said they were inferior, Mr. President," said Boyes, surprised.

"Certainly you have, John—and frequently, too."

"That's not so, sir," insisted Boyes. "No matter what you may think, I have no contempt or hatred for the Africans—which is why I've always been able to function in their countries." He paused. "I understand them—as much as any white man can. They're not inferior, but they *are* different. The things that are important to us are of no consequence to them, and the things they care about seem almost meaningless to us—and because of that, you simply can't turn them into Americans in two short years, or even twenty."

"We did it in America," said Roosevelt stubbornly.

"That's because your blacks were being assimilated into a dominant society that already existed and was in possession of the country," answered Boyes. "The whites here are just passing through, and the Africans know it, even if the whites don't. They may have to put up with us temporarily, but we won't have any lasting effect on their culture." He paused as Roosevelt considered his words, then continued: "When all is said and done, it's their country and their continent, and one of these days they're going to throw us all out. But what follows us won't look anything like a Western society; it'll be an African society, shaped by and for the Africans." He smiled wryly. "I wish them well, but personally I wouldn't care to be part of it."

"I've said it before, John: you're a very interesting man," said Roosevelt, a strange expression on his face. "Please continue."

"Continue?" repeated Boyes, puzzled.

"Tell me why you wouldn't care to be part of an African nation based on African principles and beliefs."

"For the same reason that they have no desire to become Americans or Europeans, once we stop bribing them to pretend otherwise," answered Boyes. "Their culture is alien to my beliefs." He paused. "Democracy, and the Christian virtues, and the joys of literature, and a reverence for life: all these things work for you, sir, because you have a deep and abiding belief in them. They won't work here because the people of the Congo *don't* believe in them. They believe in witch doctors, and tribalism, and polygamy, and rituals that seem barbaric to me even after a quarter century of being exposed to them. We couldn't adapt to their beliefs any more than they can adapt to ours."

"Go on, John," said Roosevelt, his enthusiasm mounting.

Boyes started at him curiously. "You've got that look about you, Mr. President."

"What look?"

"The same one I saw that first night we met in the Lado Enclave," said Boyes.

"How would you describe it?" asked Roosevelt, amused.

"I'd call it the look of a crusader."

Roosevelt chuckled with delight. "You're a very perceptive man, John," he said. "By God, I wish I were a drinking man! I'd celebrate with a drink right now!"

"I'll be happy to have two drinks, one for each of us, if you'll tell me what you're so excited about, Mr. President," said Boyes.

"I finally understand what I've been doing wrong," said Roosevelt.

"And what is that, sir?" asked Boyes cautiously.

"Everything!" said Roosevelt with a hearty laugh. "Lord knows I've had enough discussions on the subject with you and the others, but I've always proceeded on the assumption that I was part of the solution. Well, I'm not." He paused, delighted with his sudden insight. "I'm part of the problem! So are you, John. So are the British and the French and the Portuguese and the Belgians and everyone else who has tried to impose their culture on this continent. That's what you and Mickey Norton and Charlie Ross and all the others have been telling me, but none of you could properly articulate your position or carry it through to its logical conclusion." He paused again, barely able to sit still. *"Now* I finally see what we have to do, John!"

"Are you suggesting we leave?" asked Boyes.

Roosevelt shook his head. "It's not that simple, John. Eventually we'll have to, but if we leave now, the Belgians will just move back in and nothing will have changed. It's our duty—our holy mission, if you will—to make sure that doesn't happen, and that the Congo is allowed to develop free from all external influences, including ours."

"That's a mighty tall order, sir," said Boyes. "For instance, what will you do about the missionaries?"

"If they've made converts, they're here at the will of the people, and they've become part of the process," answered Roosevelt after some consideration. "If they haven't, eventually they'll give up and go home."

"All right," said Boyes. "Then what about—?"

"All in good time, John," interrupted Roosevelt. "We'll have to work out thousands of details, but I feel in my bones that after two years of false starts, we're finally on the proper course." He paused thoughtfully. "Our first problem is what to do with Billy Pickering."

"If you're worried about the Belgians, we can't give him a trial by jury," said Boyes. "These people have hated the Belgians for decades. They'll find him innocent of anything more serious than eliminating vermin, and probably vote him into the Presidency."

"No, we can't have a jury trial," agreed Roosevelt. "But not for the reason you suggest."

"Oh?"

"We can't have it because it's a Western institution, and that's what we're going to eradicate— unless and until it evolves naturally."

"Then do you want to execute him?" asked Boyes. "That might satisfy the Belgians."

Roosevelt shook his head vigorously. "We're not in the business of satisfying the Belgians, John." He paused thoughtfully. "Have Yank Rogers escort him to the nearest border and tell him never to return to the Congo. If the Belgians want him, let *them* get him."

Having summarily eliminated the system of justice that he had imposed on the country, Roosevelt spent the remainder of the week eagerly dismantling the rest of the democracy that he had brought to the Congo.

XIII

Roosevelt was sitting beneath the shade of an ancient baobab tree, composing his weekly letter to Edith. It had been almost three weeks since he had embraced his new vision for the future of the Congo, and he was discussing it enthusiastically, in between queries about Kermit, Quentin, Alice, and the other children.

Boyes sat some distance away, engrossed in Frederick Selous' latest memoirs, which had been personally inscribed to Roosevelt, whose safari he had arranged some three years earlier.

Suddenly Yank Rogers walked up the broad lawn of the state house and approached Roosevelt.

"What is it, Yank?"

"Company," he said with a contemptuous expression on his face.

"Oh?"

"Our old pal, Silva," said Rogers. "You want me to bring him to your office?"

Roosevelt shook his head. "It's too beautiful a day to go inside, Yank. I'll talk to him right here."

Rogers shrugged, walked around to the front of the building, and returned a moment later with Gerard Silva.

"Hello, Mr. Silva," said Roosevelt, getting to his feet and extending his hand.

"*Ambassador* Silva," replied Silva, shaking his hand briefly.

"I wasn't aware that Belgium had sent an Ambassador to the Congo Free State."

"My official title is Ambassador-at-Large," said Silva.

"Well, you seem to have come a long way since you were an assistant governor of an unprofitable colony," said Roosevelt easily.

"And *you* have come an equally long way since you promised to turn the Congo into a second America," answered Silva coldly. "All of it downhill."

"It's all a matter of perspective," said Roosevelt.

There was an uneasy silence.

"I have come to Stanleyville for two reasons, Mr. Roosevelt," said Silva at last.

"I was certain that you wouldn't come all this way without a reason," replied Roosevelt.

"First, I have come to inquire about the man, Pickering."

"Mr. Pickering was deported as an undesirable some nineteen days ago," answered Roosevelt promptly.

"Deported?" demanded Silva. "He killed four Belgian soldiers!"

172

"That was hearsay evidence, Mr. Silva," responded Roosevelt. "We could find no eyewitnesses to confirm it."

"Pickering himself admitted it!"

"That was why he was deported," said Roosevelt. "Though there was insufficient evidence to convict him, we felt that there was every possibility that he was telling the truth. This made him an undesirable alien, and he was escorted to the border and told never to return.

"You let him go!"

"We deported him."

"This is totally unacceptable."

"We are a free and independent nation, Mr. Silva," said Roosevelt, a hint of anger in his high-pitched voice. "Are you presuming to tell us how to run our internal affairs?"

"I am telling you that this action is totally unacceptable to the government of Belgium," said Silva harshly.

"Then should Mr. Pickering ever confess to committing a murder within the borders of Belgium, I am sure that your government will deal with it in a manner that is more acceptable to you." Roosevelt paused, as Boyes tried not to laugh aloud. "You had a second reason for coming to Stanleyville, I believe?"

Silva nodded. "Yes, I have, Mr. Roosevelt. I bring an offer from my government."

"The same government that is furious with me for deporting Mr. Pickering?" said Roosevelt. "Well, by all means, let me hear it."

"Your experiment has been a dismal failure, Mr. Roosevelt," said Silva, taking an inordinate amount of pleasure in each word he uttered. "Your treasury is bankrupt, your railroads and highways will never be completed, your bridges and canals do not exist. You have failed to hold the national election that was promised to the international community. Even the small handful of men who accompanied you at the onset of this disastrous misadventure have deserted you." Silva paused and smiled. "You must admit that you are in an unenviable position, Mr. Roosevelt."

"Get to the point, Mr. Silva."

"The government of Belgium is willing to put our differences behind us."

"How considerate of them," remarked Roosevelt dryly.

"If you will publicly request our assistance," continued Silva, "we would be willing to once again assume the responsibility of governing the Congo." He smiled again. "You really have no choice, Mr. Roosevelt. With every day that passes, the Congo retreats further and further into insolvency and barbarism."

Roosevelt laughed harshly. "Your government has a truly remarkable sense of humor, Mr. Silva."

"Are you rejecting our offer?"

"Of course I am," said Roosevelt. "And you're lucky I don't pick you up by the scruff of the neck and throw you clear back to Brussels."

"Need I point out that should my government decide that the Congo's vital interests require our presence, you have no standing army that can prevent our doing what must be done?"

Roosevelt glanced at his wristwatch. "Mr. Silva," he said, "I'm going to give you exactly sixty seconds to say good-bye and take your leave of us. If you're still here at that time, I'm going to have Mr. Boyes escort you to the nearest form of transportation available and point you toward Belgium."

"That is your final word?" demanded Silva, his face flushing beneath his deep tan.

"My final word is for King Albert," said Roosevelt heatedly. "But since I am a Christian and a gentleman, I can't utter it. Now get out of my sight."

Silva glared at him, then turned on his heel and left.

Roosevelt turned to Boyes, who was still sitting in his chair, book in hand. "You heard?" he asked.

"Every word of it." Boyes paused and smiled. "I wish he'd have stayed another forty seconds." He got to his feet and approached Roosevelt. "What do you plan to do about the Belgians?"

"We certainly can't allow them back into the country, that much is clear," said Roosevelt.

"How do you propose to stop them?"

Roosevelt lowered his head in thought for a moment, then looked up. "There's only one way, John."

"Raise an army?"

Roosevelt smiled and shook his head. "What would we pay them with?" He paused. "Besides, we don't want a war. We just want to make sure that the Congo is allowed to develop in its own way, free from all outside influences."

"What do you plan to do?" asked Boyes.

"I'm going to return to America and run for the Presidency again," announced Roosevelt. "Bill Taft is a fat fool, and I made a mistake by turning the country over to him. I'll run on a platform of making the Congo a United States Protectorate. *That* ought to make the Belgians think twice before trying to march in here again!" He nodded his head vigorously. "That's what I'll have to do, if these people are ever to develop their own culture in their own way." His eyes reflected his eagerness. "In fact, I'll leave this afternoon! I'll take Yank with me; I'm sure I can find a place for him in Washington."

"You realize what will happen if you lose?" said Boyes. "The Belgians will march in here five minutes later."

"Then there's no time to waste, is there?" said Roosevelt. "You're welcome to come along, John."

Boyes shook his head. "Thank you for the offer, Mr. President, but there's still a few shillings to be made here in Africa." He paused. "I'll stay in Stanleyville until you return, or until I hear that you've lost the election."

"A little more optimism, John," said Roosevelt with a grin. "The word *lose* is not in our lexicon."

Boyes stared at him for a long moment. "You mean it, don't you?" he said at last, as the fact of it finally hit home. "You're really going to run for the Presidency again."

"Of course I mean it."

"Don't you ever get tired of challenges?" asked Boyes.

"Do you ever get tired of breathing?" replied Roosevelt, his face aglow as he considered the future and began enumerating the obstacles he faced. "First the election, then Protectorate status for the Congo, and then we'll see just what direction its social evolution takes." He paused. "This is a wonderful experiment we're embarking upon, John."

"It'll be interesting," commented Boyes.

"More than that," said Roosevelt enthusiastically. "It'll be bully—just bully!"

The date was April 17, 1912.

XIV

AFTER RETURNING HOME FROM THE CONGO, THEODORE Roosevelt was denied the Republican nomination for President in 1912. Undaunted, he formed the Bull Moose Party, ran as its presidential candidate, and was believed to be ahead in the polls when he was shot in the chest by a fanatic named John Chrank on October 14. Although he recovered from the wound, he was physically unable to campaign further and lost the election to Woodrow Wilson, though finishing well ahead of the seated Republican President, William Howard Taft. He lost what remained of his health in 1914 while exploring and mapping the River of Doubt (later named the Rio Teodoro) at the behest of the Brazilian government, and never returned to Africa. He died at his home in Sagamore Hill, New York, on January 6, 1919.

John Boyes made and lost three more fortunes in

British East Africa, spent his final days driving a horse-drawn milk wagon in Nairobi, and died in 1951.

The Belgian Congo (later renamed Zaire) was granted its independence in 1960, and held the first and only free election in its history. This was followed by three years of the most savage inter-tribal bloodletting in the history of the continent.

THE TOR DOUBLES

Two complete short science fiction novels in one volume!

Buy them at your local bookstore or use this handy coupon:
Clip and mail this page with your order.

Publishers Book and Audio Mailing Service
P.O. Box 120159, Staten Island, NY 10312-0004

Please send me the book(s) I have checked above. I am enclosing $_____
(please add $1.25 for the first book, and $.25 for each additional book to
cover postage and handling. Send check or money order only—no CODs.)

Name _____

Address _____

City _____ State/Zip _____

Please allow six weeks for delivery. Prices subject to change without notice.

THE BEST IN SCIENCE FICTION

GREG BEAR